A Surprise in the Dark

Stephanie made her way down to the docks. She swung her flashlight around and checked all the boats. They were all tied close to shore for the night. Then she brushed some sand off her leg and started for the cabin.

She had taken only a few steps when she heard something rustling in the trees. She stopped to listen and strained to see into the woods. *It's probably just the wind. Nobody would be down here this late.*

She took another step and saw a figure moving in the shadows under the boathouse light. She went to check it out—and her breath caught in her throat as someone grabbed her right arm.

"Stephanie?"

"Luke!" she cried.

FULL HOUSE: Stephanie novels

Phone Call from a Flamingo
The Boy-Oh-Boy Next Door
Twin Troubles
Hip Hop Till You Drop
Here Comes the Brand-New Me
The Secret's Out
Daddy's Not-So-Little Girl
P.S. Friends Forever
Getting Even with the Flamingoes
The Dude of My Dreams
Back-to-School Cool
Picture Me Famous
Two-for-One Christmas Fun
The Big Fix-up Mix-up
Ten Ways to Wreck a Date
Wish Upon a VCR
Doubles or Nothing
Sugar and Spice Advice
Never Trust a Flamingo
The Truth About Boys
Crazy About the Future
My Secret Secret Admirer
Blue Ribbon Christmas
The Story on Older Boys

My Three Weeks as a Spy
No Business Like Show Business
Mail-Order Brother
To Cheat or Not to Cheat
Winning Is Everything
Hello Birthday, Good-bye Friend
The Art of Keeping Secrets

Club Stephanie:

#1 Fun, Sun, and Flamingoes
#2 Fireworks and Flamingoes
#3 Flamingo Revenge
#4 Too Many Flamingoes
#5 Friend or Flamingo?
#6 Flamingoes Overboard!
#7 Five Flamingo Summer
#8 Forget It, Flamingoes!
#9 Flamingoes Forever?
#10 Truth or Dare
#11 Summertime Secrets

Available from MINSTREL Books

FULL HOUSE™ C L U B
Stephanie

Summertime Secrets

Based on the hit Warner Bros.
TV series

Kathy Clark

A Parachute Press Book

A MINSTREL® BOOK

Published by POCKET BOOKS
New York   London   Toronto   Sydney   Singapore

A MINSTREL PAPERBACK *Original*

 A Minstrel Book published by
POCKET BOOKS, a division of Simon & Schuster Inc.
1230 Avenue of the Americas, New York, NY 10020

A PARACHUTE PRESS BOOK

 Copyright © and ™ 2000 by Warner Bros.

ISBN: 0-671-04192-4

First Minstrel Books printing July 2000

10 9 8 7 6 5 4 3 2 1

A MINSTREL BOOK and colophon are registered trademarks of Simon & Schuster Inc.

Printed in the U.S.A.

Summertime Secrets

CHAPTER
1

◆ ◄ ▪ ◆

Happy CIT to you, happy CIT to you . . . the new CIT is Stephanie . . . Happy counseling to you!" Allie Taylor's voice warbled as she held the last note longer than everyone else.

"No way!" Stephanie Tanner said. She couldn't have been more surprised by her friends. She thought she was meeting them at the Camp Sail-Away Lodge to pick up her new cabin assignment. Instead they were all standing in front of her with a frosted chocolate cake!

When Stephanie arrived at camp ten days earlier, all the CIT spots had been filled. She applied too late. Recently she got a CIT job, just like the ones her friends had, by winning a competition.

"How did you guys pull this cake off?" Stephanie asked as she pulled her long blond hair back from her face. She was wearing a bright blue sleeveless T-shirt and khaki cargo shorts. "When did you find the time? And since when are we allowed to bake in the camp kitchen?"

"We kind of got Irma to help," Darcy Powell said. Darcy was one of Stephanie's best friends from back home. She had black hair and brown skin, and she was the most loyal friend Stephanie had ever had—next to Allie, anyway.

"In fact, Irma and I kind of bonded after I burned the first one." Darcy laughed. Irma was the baker for Camp Sail-Away, where Stephanie and her friends were spending the summer.

"And after burning the second one, we were *really* close friends!" Kayla Norris added as she adjusted the clip holding her long dark-blond hair. "She even let us test the frosting."

"I can't imagine that," Stephanie said. Irma had a reputation for being gruff. Her breads and rolls were fantastic, though, so nobody minded.

"It's true," Anna Rice insisted. "She loves us now. She even asked if we'd help her design a cake for Wild and Wacky Water Day!"

The upcoming event was an annual camp tradition in which campers competed in both silly and serious races on the waterfront. The lake was her favorite place to be, so Stephanie couldn't wait for the day to happen.

"Actually, she asked *Anna* to help her design it," Darcy corrected her. "After she saw her artistic job on this."

Stephanie admired the cake. In colored frostings, Anna had drawn a girl seated in a sailboat heading across a lake. "You even managed to make it look windy," Stephanie said. She totally admired Anna's artwork, whether her friend was designing clothes, painting, or making pots in the pottery shed. "This is so cool!"

"Thanks," Anna said as she took a little bow. "It was nothing. Really."

As Darcy cut the cake and served it on paper plates, Stephanie smiled at her friends. She knew they were making an extra effort to cheer her up because of what had just happened with Luke Hayes.

Since she had arrived at camp, Stephanie was dating Luke, who was fifteen and a camper at Camp Clearwater, the "brother" camp to Camp Sail-Away. They had met one day on the lake when Luke was water-skiing; they hit it off immediately. Stephanie was completely crazy about him—or at least she thought she was.

A few nights earlier, an incident at the boys' camp had shown her Luke wasn't such a nice guy after all. The boys' lodge was vandalized, and Luke was the number one suspect. Stephanie hadn't believed Luke could be involved—until she herself found evidence that he was! Stephanie felt she could never trust Luke again.

"Here you go." Darcy handed Stephanie a piece of chocolate cake and a fork.

"Thanks." Stephanie took the plate from her and pushed any thoughts about Luke out of her mind. *Thinking about him won't help*, she scolded herself. *You're at Sail-Away this summer to hang out with your friends—not mope about a boy!*

"Mmm . . . this cake is delicious," she said.

"I agree. Yum," Allie said, her green eyes sparkling. "So, are you guys ready to get your new cabin assignments?" The CITs had spent the first week of camp in temporary assignments. Now that the camp directors knew them better, the CITs were getting their permanent assignments.

Stephanie nodded. "I can't wait. I hope I get a cabin with easy kids."

"There's no such thing, is there?" Kayla asked with a laugh.

"No, probably not," Stephanie agreed. "But I can hope, right?"

"I want the Tiger Cabin," Anna said. "I really like a bunch of the seven-year-olds I've met teaching arts and crafts."

Stephanie licked frosting off her fork. "I don't care what cabin I get—just as long as I don't have to share it with Rene, or any other Flamingo!"

Stephanie had spent the past week living with Rene Salter, who was a member of the snobby Flamingo Club. Rene was a CIT, too, and she loved making life miserable for Stephanie. She had assigned Stephanie lots of extra tasks and in general made sharing a cabin with her a real pain.

"You won't," Darcy assured her. "Well, I say we go upstairs. Heather said we should come by after lunch." Mr. McCready was the camp director, and Heather O'Donnell was the assistant director. She handled most of the day-to-day tasks and supervised all the CITs and counselors. *Now* she's *someone who really enjoys being in charge*, Stephanie thought.

Kayla tried to toss her paper plate into the trash can on the porch, but she missed. "Oops!" She picked up the plate and tried again. "Well, let's go. We've had dessert, so it's officially after lunch!"

Stephanie and her friends headed inside the lodge. All their meals were served in the main floor dining room. The camp offices were located on the second floor.

"I'll put the leftover cake in the fridge and meet you guys up there," Darcy told everyone.

They went upstairs to Heather's office, and Stephanie softly knocked on the open door. "Hello? Can we come in?" she asked.

"*May* you come in. And, yes, you may. Hello, girls." Heather glanced up at the green clock on the wall. "Lunch ended half an hour ago. Where have you been?"

"Oh, just talking," Allie said. "We didn't want to rush you."

Stephanie carefully wiped a tiny bit of frosting from the corner of her mouth. She had a feeling Heather wouldn't approve of celebrations— because they were much too frivolous. Her office was so neat that it resembled a furniture show-room. Nothing was out of place, and there were at least six file cabinets lined up against one wall.

"So, um, do you have our cabin assignments?" Kayla asked shyly.

"Yes, just a moment, please." Heather sorted through a neat stack of multicolored folders on her desk. "I was hoping all the CITs would be here at the same time, but I suppose I can give out your assignments." She cleared her throat. "All right, here's what we came up with, based on a careful evaluation of your skills."

Stephanie glanced over at Darcy and smiled. Heather had a knack for making everything sound extremely serious.

"Okay, then, in alphabetical order. Kayla Norris, Sparrow Cabin. Darcy Powell, Hawk. Anna Rice, Tiger—"

"Yes!" Anna pumped her fist in the air.

"Please hold your applause," Heather said as a tiny smile curled the corners of her mouth. "Stephanie Tanner, Loon Cabin . . ."

Stephanie grinned. *Great,* she thought. *That's one of the cabins for ten-year-olds—and I already like the head counselor, Tracey.*

"And last but not least, Allie Taylor—the Dolphins!"

"Thanks, Heather!" Allie said. "I'm so excited."

"Me, too," Stephanie said.

"If you get your bags and trunks packed up and labeled, we'll re-deliver them tonight," Heather said. "So, start packing. Neatly, of course."

"Oh, of course," Darcy replied.

Stephanie stifled a laugh. Darcy had to be the most disorganized packer ever.

"I'm so glad I get to stay with my cabin," Kayla said as they headed out of the office. "I didn't want to leave."

"I can't wait to settle in at my new cabin," Stephanie said as she rushed down the stairs.

"Gee, I don't know why you'd say that," Darcy teased. "Didn't you *like* living with Rene?"

"Yes. *Didn't* you?" another voice piped up.

Stephanie found herself facing Rene at the bottom of the stairs! With Rene was Darah Judson, one of Rene's best friends.

"Oh, well—sure," Stephanie said. "It's just that I'd rather not spend my entire summer following orders."

"I never *ordered* you around," Rene said.

Stephanie rolled her eyes. "Yeah, right."

"I just strongly suggested you do what I said." Rene laughed. "So, anyway, Stephanie, have you heard the good news?" she asked.

"Rene! It's not good news," Darah corrected her.

"It isn't?" Rene asked.

Darah shook her head. "No. It's *great* news."

"What are you guys talking about?" Stephanie demanded.

Rene giggled as she turned back to Stephanie with a wicked smile. "Guess who got kicked out of camp this morning?"

"Wait—don't tell me!" Stephanie said excitedly. "You?"

Rene glowered at her. "Hardly. I'm talking about Luke Hayes—you know, your boyfriend?"

CHAPTER
2

Stephanie felt as if she had been punched in the stomach. Tears filled her eyes as she stared at Rene.

"He's not my boyfriend," she managed to get out. *At least, not anymore.*

"Good thing," Rene said. "Because for a while there, I thought your taste in boyfriends was really slipping."

"Can you imagine—picking Luke? Out of all the cute guys here?" Darah shook her head. "He's practically a criminal."

"I know," Rene agreed.

While they bad-mouthed Luke, Stephanie grit her teeth. She was determined not to cry in front

10

of them. All she could think about, though, was how angry she was at Luke.

During a party for the boys' and girls' camps, somebody had gone to the Camp Clearwater Lodge and spray-painted the walls, turned over furniture, and trashed the place. Everyone suspected Luke right off, because he had been responsible for some camp vandalism the summer before. Stephanie didn't believe Luke was responsible. Then she saw spray paint on his T-shirt and in his cabin, linking him to the crime.

How could he do such a stupid thing? How could he ruin his summer—and hers—like that? *I can't believe he left without even saying good-bye. I'm so mad at him!*

"Why don't you leave Stephanie alone?" Darcy asked. "If Luke really is gone, then there's no point standing around bashing him."

"Anyway, Luke isn't a terrible person, the way you're making him sound," Anna said. "Did you ever consider that maybe this was a practical joke?"

"Some *joke*," Darah scoffed. "He ruined the boys' lodge! Of course, if you want to go out with that kind of person, feel free."

"I don't care what you guys say," Rene declared

as the rest of her friends, the Flamingoes, came up behind her.

"What you guys say about what?" Jenny Lyons asked. Jenny's stepfather was Mr. McCready, the director of Camp Sail-Away.

"We were talking about Luke Hayes," Darah explained. "They actually made a pathetic attempt to *defend* him." She rolled her eyes.

"Luke's bad news, and now everyone knows it," Jenny said. "My dad said so at the beginning of camp. Remember when I tried to warn you?" she asked Stephanie. "But, no, you wouldn't listen."

"Why would we listen to anything you said?" Anna shot back.

"It's not like I would take your advice," Stephanie said. "Usually when you warn us about a boy, it means you want to go out with him yourself."

"That *does* sound familiar," Darcy said as she glared at Rene.

"That's life. Not everyone can have the perfect boyfriend—Keith. It just so happens that I do." Rene smiled.

"That's because you stole him from me," Darcy said angrily.

Darcy and Keith had hit it off when they met at camp, and Stephanie was sure Keith was interested in Darcy. But as soon as Rene found out about Keith, she pushed Darcy aside and went after him herself. At the dance Rene had hogged all of Keith's time.

"She didn't steal him from you," Tiffany said. "He just happens to like her more than he likes you. Sorry!" She shrugged. "Of course, he's not as cute as Taylor. . . ."

"His name's Tyler," Rene corrected her. "The guy you met at the dance is named Tyler."

"Oh. Right," Tiffany said with a dreamy sigh.

Stephanie groaned and looked at her friends. "Let's get out of here—before we get sick."

"We were leaving, anyway," Cynthia said. "We're going upstairs to get our cabin assignments. And I bet you anything they'll be *better* than yours." She headed upstairs, and her friends all followed.

"How can they be better?" Anna asked as they walked outside. "We like all the kids here. There's no such thing as a bad cabin."

"Sorry about Rene taking Keith away from you," Allie told Darcy.

"Don't worry, he'll see what Rene is really like

very soon," Stephanie said. "Then he'll wish he never broke that date with you to go out with her."

"I'm not counting on it," Darcy said. "You know how the Flamingoes are—they don't give up without a fight. Especially when it comes to boys!"

Later that afternoon, Stephanie went down to the lake for a special meeting with the other waterfront CITs. In her new CIT job, she would be teaching sailing, windsurfing, canoeing, swimming, and water safety. Kayla and Allie were at the meeting, too, along with Rene and Jenny. The counselors and CITs from the boys' camp were also there. Though the camps had separate swimming areas and docks, they shared a boathouse and several boats.

The meeting was being held on the sandy beach area. Stephanie took a seat next to Allie and Kayla. Just before the meeting started, Max, a CIT, ran up and dropped into the sand on the other side of her.

Stephanie had met Max the same day she met Luke, on her first day of camp. She had been out in a canoe when they sped by in a motorboat and tipped her over. Luke was a great water-skier, even better than Max. Max was medium height, with curly brown hair. He was cute, but he wasn't half as good-looking as Luke, in Stephanie's opinion.

Don't think about Luke, she scolded herself as a picture of Luke's gorgeous face flashed in her mind. She remembered how he had swum toward her the first time they met, and how cute he looked, with his green eyes and wet blond hair. She thought about the time they had gone for a bike ride and how they kissed afterward, in the middle of a rainstorm.

Stop it! You have to forget him, Stephanie told herself. It wasn't working, though.

"Hey," Max said softly. "How's it going?" He scooted a little closer to Stephanie.

"Hi," Stephanie replied.

"Okay, everyone, listen up. Are you ready for the twenty-third annual Wild and Wacky Water Day?" Keira, the head counselor for waterfront activities, asked.

Everyone cheered and whistled.

"As you know, the event is only about five days away," Keira said. "That doesn't give us much time, but then, that's part of the plan. We wouldn't want anyone to be *too* prepared, right? Okay, let me tell you what's going on. First off, we have our wild events: a marathon swim race, a kayak sprint, and a diving competition—"

"Bo-ring!" someone in the crowd called out.

Keira smiled. "And then we have our wacky events. The Best Belly Flop contest, which is pretty self-explanatory. Then there's Swim-in-the-Shallows. You swim in water about two feet deep, and the person who can make it to the finish line without touching bottom wins," Keira explained. "And there's the One-Oared Rowboat Race. Does anyone out there realize how hard it is to get anywhere when you're spinning in circles?" She grinned. "I typed up a list of all the events and the details for competing. You can review them, and we'll decide who will judge and time each event.

"Now, for the group events category," Keira continued. "We have the swim relay—teams of eight have to come up with eight different styles of strokes in order to win. Then there's the Silly Sailboat Race. Cabins participate as a whole, using a theme. Since everyone has to sail, and some sail solo, this is strictly a category for campers age ten and up. And last but not least . . .

the counselors put on a synchronized swimming show that's as goofy as all these events put together!" Keira looked around the group. "Any questions?"

"Does everyone have to compete?" Allie asked. "Some campers don't like water sports."

"You're exactly right. So only those who want to compete will," Keira said. "After all, those of us out there making complete fools of ourselves need spectators."

A camper with a blond ponytail came up beside Keira. "I'm sorry to bother you, Keira," the girl said, "but could you come over here for a second? We're trying to take a sailboat out, and the rudder's stuck in the up position."

"That won't help much, will it?" Keira said with a smile. "Okay, everyone, read the handouts while I'm gone. When I get back, you can let me know what you think you'd like to do!" Keira called over her shoulder.

Stephanie reached for the stack of handouts Max handed to her and took a sheet. Then she passed them to Allie.

"Hey, I just heard about Luke being asked to leave camp," Max said softly. "Sorry."

Stephanie turned to him and shrugged. Luke

and Max weren't exactly friends—in fact, Max had tried to warn Stephanie about Luke. Stephanie had been angry with him at the time, but now she realized he was probably just a nice guy.

Still, she didn't really want to get into discussing Luke again. She wanted to read the handout before Keira came back.

"I know you liked him, but he was definitely trouble. You'll be better off without him—honest," Max told her.

Stephanie wasn't so sure about that—not yet. It was nice of Max to commiserate with her, though. "Thanks," she said.

"Don't worry—the summer can still be a blast," Max said. "Like this show next weekend? I did almost every event last year. It's so much fun."

"I can't wait," Stephanie told him. "It sounds exciting."

"It is. You know what? You should go for the all-around title," Max said. "I am!"

"I didn't know they had an award like that," Stephanie said.

"Oh, yeah—they award one girl and one guy. It's really fun going for it. Not that I've ever *won*,

18

because Luke always did, but . . ." Max flexed his tan arm. "There's hope, right?"

"Definitely," Stephanie told him with a laugh as she reached out to squeeze his biceps. "Is there a weight-lifting event, though? I thought it was all sailing and swimming."

"Yeah, too bad. Well, I can always do one of those handstand dives off the dock!" Max laughed.

"Oh, sure. I think I'll do a triple-twisting somer-sault myself," Stephanie said. "You know, just to make *sure* I belly flop."

Max burst out laughing. "Now that I have to see!"

Stephanie grinned. Talking to Max made her look forward to the waterfront show. So what if Luke wasn't around anymore? There were lots of other people to have fun with—like her friends, and her new cabin of campers, and Max.

Keira came back to the group and clapped her hands together. "Okay, everyone—listen up," she said. "Let's go around the circle and tell me what you'd like to help with."

As she waited for her turn, Stephanie heard a motorboat go by, close to the shore. She turned to the left and saw a blond-haired boy driving the boat. When he caught her eye, he turned to her and waved.

Luke! Stephanie thought angrily as her heart started to beat faster. *What are you doing here?*

You've been kicked out of camp—and I'm not supposed to see you again!

CHAPTER
3

◆ ◄ ◢ ◆

I can't believe Luke rode by during the meeting,"
Allie commented after the meeting broke up.
"What do you think he was doing—trying to get
your attention?"

"If he was, it worked!" Stephanie remembered
how shocked she had been to see him.
Shocked . . . and excited, too.

"Too bad his family lives on the lake," Kayla said.
"You'll probably see him around all summer."

Stephanie nodded. That was definitely going to
be awkward! Especially when she didn't know
how she felt about Luke. Half the time she was
mad at him . . . and half the time she wished they
were still together.

Stephanie, Kayla, and Allie were heading for the path to the cabins when Keira rushed after them.

"Stephanie, do you have a second? I want to talk to you," Keira said.

"Sure," Stephanie said. "What is it?"

"Well, I was wondering if you could take over a responsibility for me," Keira said. "It's pretty important, but I've seen and heard good things about your skills, so I think you can handle it."

"Stephanie's a pro," Allie put in.

"What is it?" Stephanie asked.

"At the end of the day—well, throughout the day, too, but at night it's most important—I need you to check all the boats to make sure they're securely tied up," Keira said. "Once in a while, we lose one, when the wind's strong and when someone didn't tie a good enough knot. We don't want that to happen."

"No problem," Stephanie said with a smile. "I'm really good at knots. I'd love to take care of that."

"Great. You can start tonight, okay? I have to warn you—last year there was someone from the boys' camp who untied them all one night. That hasn't happened so far this year, but you never know," Keira said.

Max had told Stephanie that Luke was the one who had cut the boats loose. The boys' camp director, Mr. Davis, had given Luke a second chance. *Which he ruined,* Stephanie thought.

"Okay, I'll look out for that," she said awkwardly.

"Thanks, Stephanie!" Keira ran back toward the lake.

"Wow. That's a big responsibility," Kayla commented as they resumed walking toward the cabins. "Keira really trusts you!"

"She can tell that Stephanie is gifted when it comes to boats and tying knots and all that stuff," Allie teased.

"She did compliment me on my first day here," Stephanie mused. "I guess I made a good first impression. Well, here I am." She stopped outside Loon Cabin. "Wish me luck!"

"Good luck—and have fun," Allie said. "See you at dinner."

"Good luck to you guys, too!" Stephanie waved good-bye and opened the door of the cabin.

"Stephanie!" Tracey cried. "You're here!"

"Hi!" Stephanie smiled as she looked around the cabin. All of the campers had jumped up and were standing under a banner that said, WELCOME,

STEPHANIE! The banner was draped from two pine bunk beds.

"Welcome to Loon Cabin!" the campers shouted. A few of them started making a low hooting loon call.

"Everyone calls this place the Loony Bin," Tracey whispered to Stephanie behind her hand. "But don't believe a word of it."

Stephanie grinned. "No problem. Anyway, I've been helping take care of my little sister Michelle for years. If you want to talk loony . . ."

Tracey laughed.

"No, not really—but I'm definitely used to ten-year-olds," Stephanie finished explaining.

"Good. Well, I'm really glad to have you here," Tracey told her. "We're all really glad—right, gang?"

Stephanie walked over and started talking with everyone as she learned all the names: Debra, Ashley, Jessica, Tammy, Anne, and Vanessa. She had almost memorized all of them when the door opened and Cynthia walked into the cabin. Right behind her was her little sister, Marguerite.

What are they doing here? Stephanie wondered. She had seen Marguerite on one of her first days at camp, in a tennis class Cynthia coached. From what she had seen, Marguerite was about as nice and friendly as her big sister—which wasn't friendly and nice at all.

"Marguerite, you're late," Tracey said. "Remember we were supposed to be here at five to meet your new CIT, Stephanie?"

Oh no! Stephanie thought. *I have Cynthia's little sister in my cabin?*

"Sorry, I forgot," Marguerite replied as she tossed a shopping bag on her bunk. "We went into town and we lost track of time. Cynthia wanted to get me a new sweater, and it took *forever* to find one."

Stephanie stared at Marguerite's bed: she had a pink blanket, a pink teddy bear, and a picture of a pink flamingo pasted to the wall. *She wants to be just like Cynthia*, Stephanie thought. *It might be really cute . . . if Cynthia wasn't Cynthia!*

"So *you're* her CIT?" Cynthia walked up to Stephanie.

Stephanie nodded. "What cabin did you get?"

"Who cares? The fact is that I wanted this one," Cynthia said. "And seeing you here makes me wish I'd made Heather give it to me!"

"I don't think Heather actually takes orders from CITs," Stephanie said.

"Well, she should," Cynthia said. "I promised Marguerite I'd be in her cabin. Look at her! She's totally upset!"

Stephanie glanced at Marguerite. She was glaring at Stephanie as if she had already decided to make her an enemy.

"I'm sure Marguerite will be okay," Stephanie said. "Look at it this way. Being separated, you guys will meet a lot more people, and—"

"You don't know what it's like," Cynthia said. "My sister and I are really close."

"I have a little sister, too," Stephanie said. "I know exactly what it's like. So, don't worry, I'll look out for Marguerite. I'll do everything I can to make sure she's having a good summer."

"You haven't even been a CIT yet," Cynthia complained. "Why couldn't she have gotten one of my friends instead of you?"

Tracey came over to them. "Cynthia, Stephanie, is there a problem? I thought you guys were talking, but now it sounds like an argument."

"Everything's fine," Stephanie said, "as far as I'm concerned."

"I was just telling Stephanie about Marguerite." Cynthia turned to her little sister and smiled. "How she needs extraspecial care. How we were supposed to be in the same cabin but Heather made a mistake."

"Oh, don't take it personally. They hardly ever put sisters in the same cabin," Tracey said with a shrug. "It's a way of letting them develop friendships on their own."

Cynthia frowned. "We don't need more friendships," she muttered under her breath.

Tracey didn't seem to hear Cynthia. "And don't worry about Marguerite," she went on. "We'll take good care of her and all the other loons. Right, Stephanie?"

Stephanie nodded. "We definitely will. I promise," she told Cynthia.

"Okay, then. Is anyone else as hungry as I am?" Tracey asked. "Let's all go to dinner! Stephanie, why don't you and Marguerite lead the way?"

Stephanie opened the door for Marguerite. "Marguerite, you want to go first?"

Marguerite frowned at Stephanie. Then she took Cynthia's hand instead, and they walked out together. Marguerite and Cynthia headed for the lodge without waiting for Tracey, Stephanie, and the rest of the cabin.

"Hey, wait up!" Stephanie called. She hurried after them.

Marguerite turned around and glared at her. "I'd rather go with my sister," she said in a snobby voice.

"Well, um, okay," Stephanie said. *But isn't Cynthia supposed to be with her own cabin right now?*

Being a counselor-in-training to a Flamingo-in-training is going to be impossible, she thought.

That night Stephanie waited until all her campers were in bed for lights-out. Then she told Tracey she'd be gone for a few minutes.

"I'm going down to the lake to check the boats," Stephanie explained. "It's a new assignment Keira gave me today."

"Okay, but hurry back," Tracey said.

"I will." Stephanie grabbed a flashlight from the wall by the door and went outside. The sky was so clear that the moon was nearly bright enough to light her way without the flashlight.

She made her way down to the docks. A brilliant light shining over the boathouse doors illuminated the docks area. There were reflectors along the edges of the docks and on top of the posts, too. Stephanie's flashlight beam bounced off the red and white reflectors.

Stephanie quickly checked the canoes, which

were tied close to shore. Then she fixed a few knots on the rowboat and sailboat lines.

Everything's in great shape, Stephanie thought as she made a last-minute survey of the beach. She swung her flashlight around and checked all the boats one more time. *No problem!* She brushed some sand off her leg and started for the cabin.

She had taken only a few steps when she heard something rustling in the trees. She stopped to listen and strained to see into the woods. *It's probably just the wind. Nobody else would be down here this late.*

She took another step and saw a figure moving in the shadows under the boathouse light. She went to check it out—and her breath caught in her throat as someone grabbed her right arm.

"Stephanie?"

"Luke!" she cried.

CHAPTER
4

♦ ◀ ◆ ♦

What are you *doing* here?" Stephanie tried to ignore the way her heart started beating faster whenever Luke was around. They moved out of the shadows, and Stephanie saw his blond hair curled around his ears. He wore faded blue jeans and a white T-shirt that showed off his golden brown skin, even in the dim light.

"Shh," Luke whispered, his hand still on Stephanie's arm. "Someone might hear us. I can't get in any more trouble, but you could."

Stephanie folded her arms in front of her. "Then why are you here?"

"Stephanie. Isn't it obvious? I had to see you,"

Luke said. "Just like I did this afternoon when I went by in the boat."

Stephanie felt herself blush. "I still can't believe you did that."

"Why not? You know I love taking risks," Luke said.

"Yeah, but that was a really dumb risk," Stephanie told him.

"What am I supposed to do—sit inside all summer? I really miss you, Stephanie," Luke went on. He took a step closer to Stephanie and reached for her hand.

Stephanie didn't know what to do. "I—I miss you, too," she stammered.

"It's really great to see you." Luke moved in even closer and took both of Stephanie's hands in his.

Stephanie took a step backward and let go of his hands. "I said I *miss* you, Luke—that doesn't mean I forgive you!"

"Forgive me? For what?" Luke asked.

"For vandalizing the lodge, what do you think?" Stephanie asked.

Luke's forehead creased. "Wait a second. Are you saying you think I actually did all that? That I spray-painted the lodge walls and trashed the tables and chairs?"

"Well . . . *yeah*," Stephanie said.

"But I didn't vandalize the lodge. I didn't have anything to do with it!" Luke said urgently.

"Then how come I found all that stuff in your cabin?" Stephanie argued.

"That wasn't mine!" Luke said angrily. "I told you that. Why don't you believe me?"

"Because I saw the evidence—with my own eyes," Stephanie said. "Don't you think I *want* to believe you're innocent?"

"So why can't you?" Luke asked.

"I did—until I saw the empty can of green spray paint under your bed and the list—" Suddenly Stephanie heard a twig snap behind her. Voices followed down the path. Stephanie's heart started pounding. What if somebody found her talking to Luke? She'd be in as much trouble as he was.

"You have to get out of here!" Stephanie told him. "Now!"

"Not until you say you believe I'm innocent," Luke said in a whisper.

"That's not going to happen," Stephanie whispered back. "Not tonight—not ever."

"Then I'll just have to convince you that I'm innocent. I'll see you again, Steph—soon," Luke said. "I promise."

Stephanie stared at him, confused. *Why does he want to see me again? Isn't it obvious I don't want to have anything to do with him?*

"This isn't over yet!" Luke brushed Stephanie's face with a quick kiss.

"Wait . . . Luke . . ." Stephanie whispered.

He vanished into the woods just as Rene and Tiffany came around a curve in the path and stood almost in front of her.

Rene stopped short, and Tiffany, who was walking behind her, crashed right into her.

"Ow!" Rene rubbed her heel. "You kicked me!"

"Sorry," Tiffany said as she rubbed her big toe.

"What are you doing out here?" Rene asked Stephanie.

Stephanie took a deep breath and tried to compose herself. She couldn't tell them she had just been talking with Luke. She hoped she didn't look as upset and confused as she felt.

"What are *you* doing out here?" she replied. "And why are you barefoot?"

"We're going—ow!" Tiffany leaped up and down holding her foot. "You stepped on my toe!"

"Sorry," Rene said, without sounding sincere. "Stephanie, I asked you first. Why are you walk-

ing out here at ten o'clock? Were you with someone? I thought I heard voices," Rene said.

"I'm out here by myself." Stephanie gestured
toward the lake. "I was checking all the boats."

"Why would you do that?" Tiffany asked.

"Do they get lonely or something?" Rene joked.
Tiffany giggled.

Stephanie rolled her eyes. "It's one of my new
responsibilities as a waterfront CIT. Do you mind?"

"Well, la-dee-da. Have fun checking your boats,
then," Rene said. "See you around!" She quickly
turned and headed back up the path.

Tiffany didn't follow her right away. "Rene,
aren't we going to—"

"Shh!" Rene said. "Come on."

What are they up to? Stephanie wondered. *Did
they see me and Luke together? I sure hope not.* She
knew the Flamingoes. They'd never keep such
juicy gossip to themselves.

The next morning Stephanie made sure everyone in the cabin did her morning chores. The only
one who resisted was Marguerite. *Naturally,*
Stephanie thought. Now that they'd all finished
and had left for their morning activities, Stephanie
got changed for her job at the waterfront. She was

giving windsurfing lessons, starting in half an hour, and lots of girls had signed up.

Stephanie threw her beach towel around her neck and happily walked out the door. She was so excited to finally be a CIT—and to be doing all the things she had planned when she came to camp.

On her way down to the lake, Stephanie passed the spot where she had stood talking to Luke. *I can't believe he sneaked on to camp property to see me.* It would almost be romantic, she thought—except that she was still furious at Luke for lying.

If only I could trust him again, she thought as she approached the lake. *I wish I could. But I can't.*

A cluster of campers and counselors stood on the docks.

They seemed to be searching for something as they peered at the lake shore.

"I don't see it," Keira said. "Does anyone else?"

"Is that it?" Allie pointed to a nearby cove.

"What are you guys looking for?" Stephanie asked with a smile as she walked up to the group.

Keira turned to her and frowned. "A sailboat is missing," she said. "Didn't you check them last night?"

CHAPTER
5

◆ ◂ ◂ ◆

"Stephanie, I'm really disappointed in you," Keira continued as the group started to disperse.

Stephanie was glad she wouldn't be yelled at in front of everybody. She could tell Keira was in a very bad mood.

"I thought you were going to keep track of all the boats," Keira said.

"I did. I checked every boat," Stephanie protested as she stared at the rope hanging into the water. "I even came down last night and double-checked. I *triple*-checked them."

"I know," Keira said in sympathy. "You told me at breakfast that everything was fine last night."

"It was." Stephanie walked the length of the dock and checked out the other boats. "Everything else is here. I don't know what happened."

Keira came up beside Stephanie. She was holding a pair of binoculars. "Neither do I, Stephanie. But try to check the lines more carefully. Here, why don't you see if you can spot the missing boat?"

"It's a sailboat, right? The one with the green-and-white sail?" Stephanie asked.

"Good memory," Keira said as Stephanie lifted the binoculars to her eyes. "But it might be hard to see because the sail won't be up. Let me know when you find the boat, and we'll figure out how to get it."

"Okay. I swear, I remember tying that boat up!" Stephanie focused the lenses and surveyed the lake. A few small motorboats were cruising at one end, while a man rowed along the opposite shore. Finally in a cove at the far end of the lake, Stephanie spotted the sailboat. "There it is!" She pointed to it and turned to Keira. "Now what?"

"Hey, what's going on?" a familiar voice behind Stephanie asked. "Are you spying on the boys' camp again?"

Stephanie turned around and saw Max standing on the dock behind her.

"Hi, Max," she said as she handed the binoculars back to Keira. "I was searching for a missing sailboat."

"What happened? Did another one run away?" Max joked.

"Actually, the boat drifted off last night," Stephanie said. "I guess it wasn't tied up properly. And it's totally my fault."

"It is? How come?" Max asked.

"I'm responsible for securing the boats at the end of each day," Stephanie said. "And it looks like I sort of blew it the first day. I promise, Keira—this won't happen again."

Keira smiled. "I know you tried hard. Sometime today we'll go over knot tying again. Don't worry about it too much. Now, if you could go get the sailboat, that would be great. Only you'll need someone to take you out there. I've got too much to do here, but maybe . . . no, Kayla has to supervise the swimming, so maybe . . ."

"I'll go with Stephanie," Max offered. "We can row out there together. I'll drop her at the sailboat, wait while she rigs it, and then she can sail it back."

"Sounds good to me," Stephanie said. "Thanks for offering to help."

"That would be great, Max," Keira said. "But don't you have something *you* have to do?"

"Kayaking—but not for half an hour," Max said. "I'll be back before then. Come on, Stephanie—let's go."

"This is so nice of you," Stephanie said as she and Max headed out on to the lake. "I'll row on the way out, since you have to row back."

"Deal," Max said. "Why do you think I offered to come along?" He stretched out in the back of the rowboat and tilted his face to the sun. "Now, this is the life."

"Don't fall asleep!" Stephanie chided. The rowing was hard work, but she was in good shape. When they reached the drifting sailboat, Max grabbed the bow. Stephanie carefully climbed on to the deck. She crawled back to the cockpit and slid in the centerboard. She quickly adjusted the rudder so that it was all the way down in the water. Then she got to work raising the sail. It wasn't easy to do while sitting in the boat, but she managed.

"Good job!" Max said in admiration. "Wow, you did all that really fast. You're amazing."

Stephanie shrugged. She felt a little embarrassed by all of Max's attention. "I spent a summer doing a lot of sailing," she explained. "On a boat much bigger than this one."

"So I should look out for you in the Silly Sailboat Race," Max said. "Okay. And I bet you'll do well in the One-Oared Rowboat Race, too."

Stephanie pulled the sail in tight so she could catch the wind as soon as Max let her go. "Don't worry," she said. "I can't win every event, right?"

Max laughed. "No, because I'm going to," he said. "Ready?"

"Ready," Stephanie said.

Max let go of the bow and started rowing back across the lake. Stephanie decided to give him some room, so she headed down the lake instead. She could tack back and forth a few times and then aim straight for the dock.

The only problem was the wind wasn't nearly as strong now as it had been fifteen minutes earlier. Stephanie was barely moving. "Come on, wind," Stephanie urged. "I have a class to teach!"

What little breeze there was kept coming from different directions. Stephanie kept adjusting the sail, but it was no use. Five minutes later the surface of the lake was smooth as glass. There was no wind.

"Oh, great," Stephanie mumbled. "I'm stranded!"

She looked around the lake and wondered what she could do. She didn't have an oar or paddle—she hadn't thought of bringing one along. Unless someone at camp noticed she was marooned, she'd be out there until the wind picked back up.

Stephanie heard a motorboat coming up behind her. She turned around. It was Luke, driving his family's boat. He was wearing a faded blue T-shirt and green soccer shorts. He had a baseball cap on over his blond hair.

Stephanie felt a familiar shiver of excitement when she saw him, but she tried to shake it off. Just because she was attracted to Luke didn't mean she could forgive him so quickly. They'd argued the night before. She didn't know whether she was happy to see him again so soon—or annoyed that he'd come to find her.

I just saw him last night—and now I'm seeing him again? Is this just a coincidence . . . or is he out here looking for me?

"Hey, Steph, need a tow?" Luke called as he stopped the boat several yards from the sailboat.

Stephanie looked up at the lifeless sail again. She did need a tow. But from Luke? If he wasn't allowed on camp property, he probably wasn't allowed to tow camp boats, either. Anyway, she didn't want to ask Luke for help. She didn't want to have anything to do with him.

Keep your distance, Stephanie told herself. *Don't get snowed by him again.*

"Actually, I think I'll wait for some wind," Stephanie said.

"Really?" Luke licked his index finger and held it up in the air. "I don't feel even a hint of a breeze. You could be out here all morning."

Stephanie shrugged and then busied herself with untying a knot in the sail line. Her hands were shaking as she struggled with it. *What's the matter with me?* she thought as she kept her hands out of Luke's sight. *Why does he make me feel so nervous?*

"Maybe I'll be stranded," she said to Luke. "But at least it's warm and sunny. I'll be okay."

"Stephanie!" Luke cried, frustrated. "Why are you being like this?"

"Like what?" Stephanie replied coolly.

"Never mind," Luke muttered. "Look, do you want me to tow you back to the docks or not? This is my final offer."

Stephanie glanced up at the motionless sail. "I appreciate the offer, but I'd better not. If anyone saw—"

"They won't," Luke said. "And if they do, this is basically an emergency."

"I don't know about *that*," Stephanie said. "Does the slowest sailing trip in history count as an emergency?"

"No, but extreme boredom does," Luke told her. "Like floating in a lake by yourself for hours on end?"

Stephanie laughed—she couldn't help herself. Luke could always make her laugh.

Then she spotted the large motorboat cruising right toward them. It was coming at them so fast, Stephanie was afraid it was going to crash right into her sailboat.

"Someone you know?" Luke asked.

"I'm not sure," Stephanie said as she peered at the boat. Then she saw the Camp Sail-Away logo painted on the front—and realized Heather was driving. Before she could tell Luke to take off, Heather had cruised up in front of them and cut the motor!

"What in the world is going on here?" Heather demanded.

CHAPTER
6

◆ ◀ ◗ ◆

What now? Stephanie thought.

"I came out here to retrieve this drifting sailboat," she told Heather. "Keira knows where I am—"

"Yes, but does Keira know you're meeting *him* on the lake?" Heather asked with a disapproving look at Luke.

"What?" Stephanie said. "I didn't plan to meet Luke. Max dropped me off, and I was trying to sail back, but I got marooned. There's no wind, so Luke offered to tow me."

"Yes, I see," Heather said. "But I still think this is very unusual. As you well know, Stephanie, campers are not allowed to associate with non-campers," she said sternly. "And what we have here is most definitely a non-camper." She pointed at Luke. "Not to mention an *ex*-camper. Who was asked to leave."

"I'm sorry," Stephanie said. "I didn't know—"

"You'd better review your rule book, then," Heather told her. "And as for you, Mr. Hayes, if I ever catch you hanging around camp again, I'll have to report you to the authorities."

Luke's jaw dropped, as if he were about to say something to Heather.

If I were him, I'd have lots to say! Stephanie thought. He could start by pointing out that he wasn't even around camp—he was on a public lake. And he lived in the same town! Stephanie felt herself getting furious on Luke's behalf.

Luke simply nodded at Heather. "I'm sorry." He turned to restart his engine. Before he left, he glanced back at Stephanie. "I'll see you later," he said. Then he turned, gunned the motor, and headed back down the lake toward his house.

Heather tossed a line to Stephanie. "Here, tie this to the handle. Make a good strong knot, then climb into the boat with me, so we'll have less to tow." She cleared her throat as she watched Stephanie make a knot. "What did he mean by that last comment?" she asked.

45

"What last comment?" Stephanie asked innocently. *The same last comment that I'm thinking about right now?*

"He said he'd see you later," Heather said. "When is later? When do you plan to meet again?"

"We don't!" Stephanie cried. "We never planned to meet today, and we definitely didn't talk about meeting some other time, either."

Heather's eyes narrowed as Stephanie climbed out of her sailboat. "What did you talk about, then?"

"About how I was going to get back to shore," Stephanie said. "He offered me a ride, but I turned him down."

"Good. Well, he'd better *not* see you later—or ever again," Heather said. "I can't stress this enough, Stephanie."

Obviously, Stephanie thought. Heather's attitude toward Luke was really starting to bug her.

"If you see Luke again, your CIT job will be in jeopardy," Heather said as she restarted the engine. She straightened the baseball cap on her head. "Next time you go sailing, bring a paddle along, and you won't need a tow from anyone."

Stephanie nodded.

46

"Least of all Luke Hayes." Heather shook her head as they started for the camp shore.

Give it a rest, Stephanie thought. Heather really had it in for Luke. *Of course, she does have good reason to be angry at him—we all do*, Stephanie realized.

They slowly cruised along, towing the sailboat behind them. Stephanie glanced down the lake toward Luke's house. She couldn't see his boat anymore.

Heather turned around for a second to check the sailboat. Stephanie smiled to let her know everything was okay.

Is everything okay? Stephanie wondered. She didn't know what to think anymore. She was mad at Heather for talking to Luke that way. She was mad at herself for getting into trouble for talking to him—she should have known better.

She did like seeing Luke, though. *He said he'd see me later. I wonder what he meant by that. Is he going to show up at camp again?*

I hope he doesn't, Stephanie thought. Seeing Luke was too much of a risk!

"Okay, everyone, listen up!" Tracey clapped her hands together for quiet. "An official Loon Cabin meeting is about to begin."

"I can't stand the excitement," Marguerite said as she patted her mouth to cover a fake yawn.

"This *is* exciting," Stephanie told her. She sat down next to Marguerite. "We're planning our event for the Wild and Wacky Water Day."

"Who came up with that dumb name?" Marguerite scoffed.

"I think it sounds like fun," Debra argued as she joined the circle sitting on the cabin's floor.

"So do I," Jessica added. "What's the plan?"

"You guys have seen the list of events posted at the lodge, right? You sign up to compete in anything you want, individually," Tracey explained. "There are only two group events, and we need to vote on whether or not we want to compete in them."

"Of course we do," Marguerite said in a snobby tone. "Everyone else is going to. We'll look stupid if we don't."

"That's not necessarily a reason to do anything," Tracey argued. "Just because everyone else might want to—"

"But we do want to," Marguerite said. "There's that sailboat race, and everyone in this cabin takes sailing, so we're ready. I mean, not everyone's as good as I—"

"I am," Vanessa interrupted.

Stephanie gave Marguerite a curious look. Two seconds ago, Marguerite had called the whole thing "babyish." Now she was bragging about what a good sailor she was.

"Well, let me explain more of what the events are, first," Tracey said. "The Silly Sailboat Race is a timed relay, and it's also an event where people get awards for best costume. We'd even decorate our boat. But everyone needs to feel comfortable sailing to do this one—and we'd be competing against a boys' cabin from Clearwater. All seven of you—plus Stephanie, because CITs compete, too."

"Let's do that one," three girls said at once.

"That sounds like fun," Marguerite agreed. "Costumes, decorations, *boys*—"

"What's not to like?" Jessica said with a giggle.

"Okay, okay, but hear me out. The other event is called the Very Individual Swim Medley. We'd each have to swim a lap and use a different stroke. After we use up the basic ones—crawl, backstroke, butterfly—"

"I cannot do the butterfly." Debra shook her head. "I've tried."

"Are you serious? It's so easy," Marguerite said.

"Not for everyone," Tracey told her. "And there's the breaststroke. Then the other four campers would have to make up their own strokes. We get judged on the creativity of the strokes, and on how long it takes us to finish the relay!" She looked around the semicircle. "So, any comments?"

"I think the sailboat race sounds like more fun," Debra said.

"Me, too," added Vanessa. "Can you imagine us all in costumes?"

"That would be totally awesome," Tammy said with a grin.

"Let's do it!" Marguerite declared.

"Stephanie, what do you think?" Tracey asked. "You have to sail, too."

"Does she really have to?" Marguerite snapped.

Stephanie couldn't believe that Marguerite still disliked her so much. *She's been brainwashed by Cynthia. It's the only explanation.*

"Marguerite! That's no way to talk," Tracey reprimanded her. "You guys are lucky to have Stephanie on your team."

"Yeah!" Vanessa said. "Stephanie's one of the best CITs there is."

"Oh." Marguerite shrugged. "Well, I just

thought it would be fun if it was only *us*. That's all."

That and the fact that your sister told you to be mean to me! Stephanie thought. "I'm definitely up for doing the sailboat race," she said to the group. "Since I'm down at the lake all day, I could *even* make sure we pick out one of the really good boats."

"Aren't they all the same?" Tracey asked.

Stephanie shook her head. "Some are newer, which means they're slightly lighter and faster."

"Cool!" Jessica said. "If we beat the boys' cabin—"

"What theme are we going to use?" Marguerite interrupted excitedly.

"First, I think we need to take a cabin vote on this, just to make sure," Tracey said. "Does every-one feel comfortable sailing alone? If not—"

"Yes!" seven girls screamed at once.

"Please let us do this—please!" Jessica said.

"Whoever wants to participate in the Very Individual Swim Medley, raise your hands," Tracey said calmly.

Stephanie looked around the circle. Nobody moved a muscle.

Tracey smiled. "Whoever wants to compete in the Silly Sailboat Race, raise *your* hands."

Seven hands waved in the air. Stephanie put hers up, too.

"Then it's settled. We'll do it!" Tracey said. "Now, all we have to do is pick a theme, which isn't going to be easy. I thought you guys could throw out some ideas, and then we'll think about them and make a decision. Sound good?"

"We're the Loon Cabin, so . . . shouldn't we have a loony boat?" Jessica suggested.

"What are you saying?" Marguerite asked with a sneer.

"We could all dress up as loons, in black and white—with little dots around our necks," Jessica said. "We could decorate the boat the same way!"

"No." Marguerite shook her head. "Are you serious? We'd never win the contest."

"Still, it's a good idea," Stephanie assured Jessica. She didn't like the way Marguerite criticized everyone.

"How about the *Titanic*?" Marguerite suggested.

"No way! You know what happened to that," Debra said. "Besides, we can't get Leonardo DiCaprio by Saturday."

Ashley laughed. "Then how about if we go as famous women in history? Like Amelia Earhart and Eleanor Roosevelt—"

"Marie Antoinette," Jessica added. "Isn't she the one who said, 'Let them eat cake!' I could wear a cake pan on my head."

"I'll dress as Cleopatra!" Debra chimed in, laughing. "Instead of riding down the Nile, I'll be sailing across Clearwater Lake!"

"Sounds great," Tracey told them with a laugh. "Any other ideas?"

"I'm going as Princess Diana," Marguerite announced. "I'll make a tiara and everything."

"You all have really good ideas," Stephanie said. "I wonder if I could dress as a famous swimmer in history—that way I'd only have to wear my swimsuit. Maybe I'll go as Esther Williams."

"Who's *that*?" Marguerite asked.

"She was a great swimmer back in the nineteen thirties, I think," Stephanie said. "And then she became a movie star. She always looked really glamorous."

"Well, for my Princess Diana costume," Marguerite cut Stephanie off, "I want a really long gown, and gloves—"

"But we'll be sailing," Vanessa reminded her.

"Vanessa's right—we should think about that," Tracey said.

"So? I can still wear gloves and a tiara,"

Marguerite said. "I'm a good enough sailor—I think I can manage to sail in a gown and satin shoes." She made it sound like the easiest thing in the world.

"You probably can," Tracey said. "But what if there's a strong wind and you have to lean way out to keep from tipping over? Then what?"

Marguerite shrugged. "Then nothing. I'll look really pretty while I do it."

Vanessa looked at Debra and rolled her eyes. Stephanie had a feeling her campers were getting sort of tired of Marguerite's superior attitude.

"Well, I have an idea," Stephanie cut in. "We could sew our costumes from really lightweight fabrics, like nylon," Stephanie said. "Something that wouldn't weigh us down and would make it easier for us to navigate the boat."

"I don't know. I was thinking we could use old costumes from previous talent shows. Sewing our own is a lot of extra work," Tracey said. "I'm not sure we'll have time. Oops—speaking of time, I have to run to a counselors' meeting. We'll finish planning the race tomorrow. Could you get everyone ready for lights-out, Stephanie? I should be back in about an hour."

"Sure thing," Stephanie replied with a smile.

"I'd be glad to help out." Tracey still trusted her, even though Keira and Heather had their doubts.

That reminds me—I won't be able to double-check the boats tonight. Well, they were all fine after dinner when I looked at them. I'll just have to hope that's enough.

Tracey dug out a sweater from her trunk. Then she grabbed a flashlight off her night table, which was a wooden orange crate turned on its end.

"Don't you want to take a raincoat?" Stephanie asked as she got to her feet. "It sounds like it's about to storm."

"Good point." Tracey grabbed a yellow slicker from a peg. "Good night, everyone—sleep well!" She slipped outside just as thunder rumbled across the sky.

"Why don't you guys get into your pajamas," Stephanie suggested. "It's almost past lights-out!"

She straightened her bed and put away some clothes while everyone brushed her teeth and got ready for bed. About fifteen minutes later everyone had slipped under the covers—except Marguerite.

"Are you guys all ready for bed?" Stephanie asked with a pointed look at Marguerite, who was pacing around the cabin.

"There's no way we'll be able to sleep through the storm," Marguerite complained. She looked out the window by her bunk.

"I know! Please, Stephanie—tell us a ghost story!" Debra begged.

There was another crack of thunder outside. Rain started to fall right afterward. It lashed against the cabin windows.

"I don't know. Isn't it scary enough for you guys already?" Stephanie asked with a smile.

"No way," Jessica said. "This is nothing."

"Anyway, what's the *point* of thunderstorms without ghost stories?" Ashley asked. "That's half the reason to come to summer camp. Am I right, guys?"

"It's not like we're six," Marguerite said as she climbed into bed. "We can handle it. *I* bet you don't even know a story we haven't heard yet."

"Oh, yeah? I bet I do," Stephanie said. She remembered a creepy story her uncle, Jesse, had once told her when he was baby-sitting her. "Okay. Everyone ready? I'm going to turn out the lights."

"Find a candle!" Debra said.

Stephanie grabbed a box of matches off the ledge by the door and lit the pillar candle they kept next to the big flashlight. She sat down on the floor and wrapped her sleeping bag around her legs to stay warm. She set the candle in front of her. The flame flickered as a draft swept through the cabin.

"Once upon a time," she began.

"Come on," Marguerite said. "Give me a break. Can't you do better than *that*?"

"Hey, give me a chance. I was just kidding!" Stephanie said. "Okay. Here's what happened. This is a true story. It's something that I actually got to see last summer," she lied. "I was staying at my grandparents' house, near the ocean. There's a lighthouse down the beach from them—a really tall, old lighthouse. A man used to live there. A hundred years ago or so. But one night, during a tremendous thunderstorm—"

Lightning flashed outside, and the cabin was flooded with light for a second. Then it went dark as the thunder rumbled. Then lightning struck again.

"It was actually a storm a lot like this one," Stephanie said. "The fog was so thick, nobody could see the lighthouse. Everyone told the light-house keeper to leave, because he wouldn't be safe there. They told him that the wind could knock the lighthouse down—it was as strong as a hurricane that night. He wouldn't leave. He refused.

"The storm hit the hardest right about midnight. Trees fell, and boats washed up onto the shore. Lightning struck all over town and set three houses on fire. The townspeople were sheltered in the town hall basement on a hill above the ocean, but they kept peering out the tiny windows to see what was happening. They all feared for their lives. The storm was at its peak when they saw a giant freighter head right for the lighthouse," Stephanie explained.

"Everyone hoped the freighter would be able to stop. But it was riding the crest of a wave. The freighter's bow did smash into the lighthouse, and it swayed back and forth before toppling to the ground. It was nothing but bits of stone!

"When the storm was over, everyone ran to see what had happened to the lighthouse keeper. Nobody could find him. They dug through all the rubble. They never found him or his body. He was never seen alive again, though, so they decided he had been swept out to sea."

Thunder cracked right above the cabin, and a few of the girls put their pillows over their ears.

Stephanie hadn't heard such loud thunder in a long time. She wondered if she should keep going.

"Go on! Tell us what happened!" Anne said.

"Well. The town had to rebuild the lighthouse," Stephanie said. She stopped as she thought she saw something moving just outside the cabin window. Stephanie got up and looked out.

Is that a branch—or is somebody out there? She wondered.

"What is it?" Vanessa asked.

"Oh, it's—um—nothing." Stephanie sat back down and continued telling the story. "So they cleared away the old one and built the new lighthouse on the same spot, which was ideal. The town hired a new keeper to operate the lighthouse. Everything went fine—until the night of the first big storm. Then suddenly, without explanation, the light went out."

There was a flash of lightning, and Stephanie saw something moving outside the window on the far side of the cabin. Stephanie watched and waited for another lightning flash to see who it was. She wouldn't admit it to her campers, but she was scared. *It's probably just Tracey, on her way back*, Stephanie tried to tell herself.

Lightning flashed and thunder cracked. Stephanie's eyes widened as she saw a familiar face at the window. *It's Luke!* Stephanie panicked. *He said he'd come to see me!*

When the lightning vanished, so did Luke.

"Stephanie, what is it?" Anne asked.

"Oh—nothing." She cleared her throat nervously and continued the story. She didn't know what else to do.

"The keeper tried everything he could to get the light to work," she continued. "As he was working in complete darkness, he felt a cold hand on the back of his neck. He looked back and saw blood dripping to the floor—"

"Aaiieeehh!"

Suddenly Marguerite let out an earsplitting shriek!

CHAPTER
7

♦ ◀ ◆ ♦

"What in the world is going on?" Tracey appeared in the doorway just as Stephanie was rushing over to Marguerite's bunk.

Tracey hurried to Marguerite's side and put her arms around her before Stephanie could get there. "It's okay," she assured her. "I'm here, and nothing will hurt you."

"But—I saw something," Marguerite said. "Stephanie was telling us this . . . this . . . *horrible* story about this dead lighthouse keeper and . . . and . . ." She started sniffling. "I saw someone outside the cabin!"

"What was it—a shadow? A person?" Tracey asked. She turned to Stephanie. "Did you see something?"

Stephanie shook her head. "No, I—I didn't see anything," she lied. She couldn't tell anyone she had seen Luke. Tracey would want to know what he was doing. *What is he doing outside on a night like this, anyway?*

"But you acted like you did," Anne reminded Stephanie. "Your face was completely pale!"

"I saw something!" Debra piped up. "I don't know if it was an animal . . . or a person . . . or *what*."

"*I* think it was a ghost," Jessica said.

And I know it was Luke! Stephanie thought nervously. If he kept this up, he was going to get *her* kicked out of camp, too. She didn't want that to happen.

"Well, I think you might have all gotten spooked by the storm. I didn't see anything when I came in. Let me check." Tracey stepped outside for a few seconds.

Stephanie kept her fingers crossed while Tracey checked. *Don't find Luke out there. Please!* she thought. When Tracey came back inside, she said, "There's nothing out there now. Maybe it was just the wind moving some branches around."

Marguerite shook her head. "No way. I *saw* someone."

"Don't worry. It could have been a counselor on

her way back from our meeting," Tracey said. "Right? It could even have been me."

Or it could have been an ex-camper named Luke, Stephanie thought. *Who doesn't know enough to stay away!*

"Stephanie, I know the girls probably begged you to tell them a ghost story," Tracey said. "But you have to use better judgment in the future and not scare them at night."

Stephanie glanced at Marguerite, who was grinning at Stephanie.

She probably only screamed because she saw Tracey coming, Stephanie thought. *And she wanted to get me in trouble!*

"I'm sure not *everyone* wanted to be that scared," Tracey continued. "Some kids don't like ghost stories, and some scare easily. It's your job to decide what's best for *everyone*."

"I told her I didn't like ghost stories!" Marguerite added.

What? Stephanie thought. *You're the one who told me "once upon a time" wasn't good enough!* But she couldn't argue with Marguerite—she'd only look worse in front of Tracey.

"Sorry," Stephanie said. "I'm really sorry, Marguerite. I won't make the same mistake again." She turned to the other campers. "You guys, I probably shouldn't have told you a ghost story tonight. I didn't mean to scare anyone," Stephanie said to Marguerite.

"Yeah, right." Marguerite turned to the wall and snuggled deeper into her sleeping bag.

"Just try to forget about it. We're all here together," Tracey told her. "And nothing's going to happen. Now, try to get some sleep—tomorrow we'll start making our costumes and figure out how to decorate our sailboat. Okay, everyone?"

"Okay," Marguerite said. She turned back toward Tracey and smiled. "Good night." Stephanie watched Marguerite happily fluff her pillow and burrow into her sleeping bag.

She only screamed to get me in trouble with Tracey! Stephanie realized. *And the worst thing is that it worked.*

What a close call, Stephanie thought as she got ready for bed. Between Marguerite's making trouble for her, and Luke's constantly turning up, Stephanie knew she was treading on thin ice. *The next time I see Luke, I'm telling him to stay away!*

After breakfast the next morning, Stephanie headed to the lake. She wanted to check out the sailboats and pick one for the Loon Cabin to use in the Silly Sailboat Race.

When she neared the docks, a familiar sight greeted her. A bunch of people were standing around. They were gazing out at the lake. Stephanie felt her heart sink. *No—don't tell me!*

She jogged up beside Max. "Is a boat missing?" she asked.

Max nodded. "Sorry. It's a rowboat this time."

"But I tied all the rowboats," Stephanie protested loudly. She hurried over to Keira. "I don't know what happened," she said. "I know I tied everything securely."

"Apparently not," Keira said. She didn't smile. "Stephanie, I told you, this assignment was important! If you can't handle the job, I can give it—"

Stephanie shook her head. "No, you don't have to do that. Hey, I just thought of something. Maybe it was the storm!" she suggested. "The wind was pretty intense last night."

"Your knots should be strong enough to withstand the wind," Keira said.

Max stepped up beside Stephanie. "I've seen Stephanie's knots," he said. "Not even Houdini could get out of them."

Keira laughed. "Well, I don't know about that."

"Seriously, Keira. She knows what she's doing," Max insisted. "You don't have to reassign the job."

Stephanie nodded, grateful for Max's support. How did he know she didn't want to lose the extra responsibility? Even if it hadn't been working out lately, she still wanted the chance to prove herself.

"I've been so careful, Keira. I don't know how the boats are getting loose," Stephanie said. "The only thing I can think of is that someone's been taking the boats out on the lake after I check them—and then not tying them up right."

"That's possible. Unlikely, but possible," Keira said. "I don't know what's going on here, but we'll get to the bottom of this. I'll talk with you later!" She headed for the boathouse.

"Hi, Steph!" Allie walked up to the docks. "Hey, can I talk to you for a minute?" She glanced at Max. "Hi."

"I'll go get some oars—we can row out and tow the rowboat back," Max offered with a smile.

Once he was gone, Allie moved closer to Stephanie. "You're not going to believe this. A really cute boy just asked me out!"

"That's great!" Stephanie said. "Who is he?"

"His name's Sam and he's fourteen. He wants me to go on a hike with him this afternoon," Allie said. "He's friends with Max, and he said maybe I could go with him, and you could go with Max."

Stephanie was just mulling over what to do, when Max returned with the two sets of oars. He handed a pair of oars to Stephanie. "Should we get going on today's rescue mission?"

Stephanie rubbed her shoulders. "I'm still sore from rowing yesterday. Did you see the runaway boat?"

"It's not far—just over there." Max pointed. "It's still floating, so that's a good sign. I was worried it might get bashed by the rocks in the storm."

"I can just see me calling home. Dad, could you buy Camp Sail-Away a new boat?" Stephanie laughed.

"Hey, Max—you're coming for a hike with me and Sam today, right? After lunch?" Allie asked.

Max nodded. "And I was about to ask Stephanie if she wanted to come with us. So, do you? We're going up Blackberry Hill—it's not a long hike, but there's a great view from the top."

"I don't know," Stephanie said. "I kind of feel like I should sit here all day and all night and watch the boats!"

"That would be a total waste of your summer," Max said. "Come on—it'll be great."

"Hey, guys." A boy with very short brown hair walked up beside Allie and smiled at her. Then he turned to Stephanie. "Hi, I'm Sam. So, are you coming with us today?"

"I want to, but—" Stephanie began.

"She said something about wanting to sit on the docks all day, playing Boat Patrol," Max said.

Stephanie laughed. "I can't help it if I'm responsible for all of these!"

"I'll go over every single boat with you before we go," Max offered. "*And* when we get back. *And* tonight. Okay?"

"Please, Steph—come!" Allie begged. "We'll have a great time." While Sam and Max started talking about the hike, Allie pulled Stephanie aside and whispered, "Max is so cute! Almost as cute as Sam. You *have* to come."

Stephanie thought it over for a minute. Allie really wanted her to go, and she did like hanging out with Max. "Okay," she finally told Allie. "Count me in!"

"Last one to the top has to carry all the gear back!" Max shouted before sprinting up the final fifty yards to the summit.

Stephanie bolted after him, determined not to let Max win. They had been hiking together for the past hour, and she didn't intend to let him beat her the last few minutes.

Stephanie and Max finished side by side. She held up her hand and he gave her a high five.

"Nice job!" Max commented.

"The sprint was easy," Stephanie said. "Hiking through all those burrs—now, that was another story." She pulled a few prickly burrs off her socks. "I think I had a hundred of these stuck to me back there."

Sam reached the top of the rocky hill next. Allie followed just a few seconds later.

"No fair! You guys had a head start," Sam said.

"I can't carry everyone's stuff!" Allie complained.

"I'll help," Sam offered. "Anyway, if we drink all the water we brought, there won't be anything to carry back down—except empty bottles. Right?"

"In that case, cheers, everyone!" Allie popped the top off her water bottle and knocked it against Sam's canteen. "Come on, have some!"

Stephanie laughed as she perched on a rock. "Allie just *loves* hiking."

"I do," Allie said. "I love the fresh air, the flowers, the views . . . everything but the actual walking uphill."

Sam smiled at her. "I think you did great. Have a seat—I'm going to look for some blueberries. I found them up here last year, so hopefully . . ."

"I'll go with you," Allie said. She and Sam wandered off.

Stephanie smiled. She was really happy Allie had found a guy she liked.

"Stephanie, come over here!" Max called. "The view is awesome."

Stephanie picked her way across the rocky summit. She had just about reached Max when she stumbled on a loose rock. She nearly plowed right into Max. He grabbed her to keep her from falling.

"Whoops!" Stephanie looked up into Max's eyes. "Sorry about that."

"No problem." Max lifted his hand to Stephanie's cheek. He traced her jaw line.

What's going on here? Stephanie wondered. *Is he about to kiss me?* Stephanie didn't know if she was ready for that. "I guess I can be kind of a klutz sometimes," she said in an attempt to lighten the conversation.

"Yeah, I guess so. Lucky for me." Max tilted

Stephanie's face and gave her a quick kiss on the lips. "Do you think you could crash into me again sometime?"

"Sure." Stephanie stepped back from Max and smiled awkwardly. Kissing Max so soon after kissing Luke made Stephanie feel strange. She couldn't help comparing the two. When she kissed Luke, the whole world seemed to vanish. There was electricity between them. She didn't feel the same thing when she kissed Max.

She had made a vow not to fall for Luke again, though. If she couldn't trust him, she didn't want to have anything to do with him. *And it's not like Heather would ever let me see Luke again, anyway,* she thought. *So maybe I should just forget him and focus on Max.*

There was one problem though. She didn't know if she could.

CHAPTER
8

◆ ◀ ◆ ◆

That night after dinner Stephanie took a seat on the lodge steps and gazed at the sun setting over the hills. "Isn't this place beautiful?" she said to her friends.

"It's great," Darcy said. "Of course, it's more *romantic* for some than for others." She gave Stephanie a funny look.

"What are you talking about?" Stephanie asked.

"We heard you guys had fun this afternoon." Kayla giggled as she poked Allie in the ribs. "Allie wouldn't stop talking about your hike when we were down at the lake afterward."

"I can't help it if Sam's cute!" Allie said. "*Really* cute."

"He is," Stephanie agreed. "And he *really* likes you, Allie."

"That's good," Allie said. "I've never been on a hiking double date before. It was awesome."

Darcy put a hand on Allie's forehead. "Do you have a fever or something? You just said hiking was awesome."

Allie grinned. "Hey, it all depends who you're hiking with! Speaking of which, you and Max seemed to be having a good time."

"We did have fun," Stephanie admitted. "He actually even kissed me."

"What?" Anna cried. "Hold on—this is not fair. I haven't met anyone so far this summer. And now you have two guys you like?" she asked Stephanie.

"I don't know if I like them both," Stephanie said. "Max is nice and everything, but I still miss Luke."

"Forget Luke," Allie said. "Max is here, and he's crazy about you."

It's not that easy, Stephanie thought. *I had really deep feelings for Luke—and maybe I still do. I don't know anymore.*

"Darcy, if only you were still dating Keith," Allie said, "then we could all go out together."

"If he didn't have really bad taste and decide to go out with Rene instead of me? Maybe I'd think about talking to him again," Darcy said. "*Maybe.*"

"But he probably doesn't deserve to talk to you," Anna said.

"Yeah," Darcy admitted. "I guess I don't like him very much anymore. I thought he was a nice guy, but . . ." She shrugged. "I'll keep looking."

"Well, it's his loss," Kayla told her. "Definitely."

"So did you make plans to see Max again?" Allie asked Stephanie eagerly.

"No, not really," Stephanie said. "I'm sure I'll see him down at the lake tomorrow. But this time I hope we won't be rescuing boats together."

"I can't believe those knots come untied *every* night," Darcy said. "It's almost like someone's taking the boats out after dark."

Stephanie hit the palm of her hand against the wooden steps. "You're so brilliant! That has to be it." Why hadn't she thought of it before? Somebody might be going out on the lake late at night. Or somebody might be untying the lines just to create trouble, or . . .

Stephanie thought of how Luke had sneaked on to camp property the past two nights. And each morning afterward, a boat was missing. *Luke can't be doing this to me . . . can he?*

"I bet Darcy's right, Stephanie. I bet someone's taking the boats out at night," Kayla said. "I really don't know who would, but . . . that has to be it."

"If I were you, I'd hide down there one night soon and see what happens," Darcy suggested. "That way, if you're there, you can catch the person in the act!"

"That's a great idea," Stephanie said. "Do you think I'd get in trouble for being out there at night, though? I mean, I really should be in my cabin."

"Ask Tracey for permission," Anna recommended. "Tell her you're determined to catch the boat thief. She can't argue with that."

"True," Stephanie said as she mulled it over. "I can't go tonight, though—it's Tracey's night off, and I'm on cabin duty until really late. And we're supposed to work on costumes for the Silly Sailboat Race all night, too!"

"Tomorrow night, then," Allie said.

"Right," Stephanie said. "I'll do my stakeout tomorrow night. In the meantime, I'd better go check the boats now. Anyone want to come?"

"I should get back to the cabin," Anna said.

"We're in the middle of eight different projects for Wild and Wacky Water Day."

"So are we!" Darcy said. "Tell me about yours."

"I can't do that," Anna said. "I've been sworn to secrecy."

"Rats," Darcy said. "And just when I needed to steal your ideas."

Stephanie laughed and waved good-bye to her friends. Then she walked down the path to the lake. She wasn't going to share her worries with her friends—not yet. But she was very afraid that her stakeout would reveal that Luke was the one who had been cutting the boats loose.

She had *seen* him outside her cabin the night before. Maybe he was sneaking back on to camp property just to cause trouble. Maybe he was doing it to get Stephanie's attention. Stephanie didn't know what would make him do it, exactly. She just knew she wanted him—or whoever it was—to stop!

Down at the waterfront, each boat was where it was supposed to be. Stephanie checked the knots and retied a couple of less-than-perfect ones.

Then she went back to her cabin and spent the evening helping her campers work on their costumes for the sailboat race. At nine o'clock she made sure everyone was in bed for lights-out. Tracey wouldn't be back until after ten. Stephanie wanted to stay awake until then, but she was exhausted after all the hiking and the swimming she had done that day.

Stephanie's eyelids drooped as she read by flashlight on her bed. *I have to stay awake*, she told herself. *I have to show Tracey I can be responsible.*

Then again, Stephanie thought, *there's no law that says I have to be awake. I just have to be here in case anything happens or anyone needs me.* She rolled over and punched her pillow a few times, then drifted off to sleep.

"Stephanie! Stephanie!"

Startled, Stephanie opened her eyes. A bright light was shining in her face. "T-Tracey?" she stammered.

"No, actually, it's *Cynthia*. I came by to say good night to Marguerite—but she's not here."

Cynthia took a step toward Stephanie. "I want to know where my sister is!"

CHAPTER
9

♦ ◀ ◆ ♦

Stephanie quickly sat up. "Maybe she went to the bathroom," she said, glancing over at Marguerite's empty bunk. Then she slipped on her flip-flop sandals and stood up.

"I already checked," Cynthia said. "She's not there, Stephanie—and I'm holding you personally responsible."

The screen door opened and Cynthia whirled around.

Tracey walked into the cabin.

"Oh. I thought maybe you were my sister," Cynthia said in a sad, dejected voice.

"Why? Where's Marguerite?" Tracey asked with a note of concern.

"I don't know, but she's definitely not here," Cynthia said. "Can you believe it? Stephanie has *no* idea where she is. It's the middle of the night!"

Tracey put a hand on Cynthia's shoulder. "Don't worry, Cynthia. Your sister will be okay."

"You should have known to keep an eye on her!" Cynthia told Stephanie. "She's been really homesick—that's why I came by to check on her. She hasn't been sleeping at all, and—"

"I'll find her," Stephanie said as she headed for the door. "Wait here, in case she comes back. But I'll find her, Cynthia—I promise!"

"You'd better," Cynthia said. "If anything happens—"

"It won't," Tracey assured her.

"This is totally Stephanie's fault. I can't believe she can't even keep track of her campers!" Stephanie heard Cynthia complain as she stepped out into the darkness. She carried a flashlight in one hand and a blanket in the other. She shined the flashlight's beam all around the outside of the cabin. Behind her she could hear other girls in the cabin, who were awake now and talking. They sounded worried.

I'm sure it's nothing. Maybe Marguerite went outside for a breath of fresh air. Maybe she sleepwalks,

Stephanie thought. *Of course, it's never happened on any other night, but that would be just my luck.*

"Marguerite?" Stephanie called softly into the night. She didn't want to wake up everyone in camp. Then again, if she didn't find Marguerite, she'd have to. She could just imagine Heather's reaction if she was woken up to join a search party.

If I were Marguerite . . . where would I go? Stephanie thought. She started walking down the path toward the lake. *Maybe she went looking for Cynthia. Maybe she has a secret hiding place.*

Suddenly Stephanie heard rustling noises behind her in the woods. She stopped moving and listened carefully. Was that a raccoon? Or a person? she wondered.

Stephanie thought she heard human footsteps off in the distance. "Marguerite?" she called. She took a few steps into the woods.

There was no answer. Stephanie walked farther into the woods. She switched off her flashlight and moved by the light of the moon. *If Marguerite is deliberately trying to hide out here, then she'll run away from me,* Stephanie thought. *Especially considering she doesn't like me very much.*

Stephanie heard another twig crunch and kept

going in the direction of the noise. She stopped as she heard a muffled squeak. Was that giggling? Was that Marguerite?

Then Stephanie recognized the giggle. She'd heard it in the woods before, a few nights ago. It was Tiffany! Stephanie held her breath and listened.

She couldn't make out the words, but she heard both Tiffany's and Rene's voices—and then she heard Marguerite's.

Marguerite's not alone out here, Stephanie realized. *She's hiding out with Rene and Tiffany—and they sent Cynthia over to the cabin to get me in trouble!*

It all makes sense now, Stephanie thought angrily. *This is all a Flamingo plot.*

She wasn't going to let them get away with it. She'd surprise them and blow their cover.

Stephanie rushed through the woods toward the voices. But when she reached the clearing, only Marguerite was there.

"Marguerite! Oh, I'm so glad I found you," Stephanie said. "Are you okay?"

"I'm fine," Marguerite said. "I mean, um, I was lost. It was really upsetting!"

"Uh-huh." Stephanie nodded. "So you were all alone out here?"

Marguerite nodded. "I was all, all alone. And I didn't know which way to go!"

"That's weird. Because I could have sworn I heard voices," Stephanie said. "Weren't you just talking to someone?"

"Me? No." Marguerite shook her head.

"Really? I thought I heard someone talking to you," Stephanie said. "It sounded like Rene and Tiffany—you know, Cynthia's friends?"

Marguerite shook her head. "It wasn't them."

"Then who was it?" Stephanie asked.

"Nobody! Look, maybe I was afraid and I was talking to myself," Marguerite said. "Maybe there were some animals in the bushes. That's probably what you heard."

"Uh-huh. Well, that explains part of it. But I still want to know why you are out in the woods, Marguerite," Stephanie said. "What are you doing?"

"Doing?" Marguerite repeated. "N-nothing. Isn't it obvious? I'm lost!"

"You said that, but I want to know why you came out here in the first place."

Marguerite crunched a twig with her sneaker. "Because I couldn't sleep, and I was going to go for a walk."

"But you know you can't leave the cabin after lights-out," Stephanie reminded her.

"I was upset," Marguerite said. "I was thinking of running away, okay?"

"Really?" Now Stephanie was truly concerned. "But you're having a good summer here, aren't you? We're doing the sailboat race, and your sister is here—" Stephanie said.

"I don't want to talk about it with *you*," Marguerite said in an unfriendly tone. "Could we just get back to the cabin? I'm freezing!"

"Sure—I'm sorry," Stephanie said. "Come on—follow me." She led Marguerite out of the woods to the path. Then they headed up the path toward Loon Cabin.

"Speaking of your sister, Cynthia's waiting for you," Stephanie told Marguerite as they approached the cabin. "She came by. She was worried about you, and when you weren't here, she kind of panicked."

"Cynthia's here?" Marguerite asked. She rushed ahead to the front door and threw it open.

"Marguerite!" Cynthia shrieked. "Oh, I'm so glad you're all right!" She ran over to her little sister and threw her arms around her. "*Are* you all right?" she asked as she held Marguerite at arm's length and studied her face. "Oh no, a scratch!"

"I think I cut myself on a branch." Marguerite sniffled. "I was so—so scared," she stammered. "And then I got lost and—"

"Why did you go out there in the first place?" Tracey asked.

"I, um . . ." Marguerite hesitated.

"It's okay," Cynthia said, her arm on Marguerite's shoulder. She squeezed Marguerite and whispered something in her ear.

"I thought I heard a bear growling," Marguerite said.

"No!" Cynthia gasped.

Stephanie thought she was going to be sick. Wasn't it obvious to Tracey that Cynthia was coaching Marguerite through this whole thing? Now Marguerite was giving Tracey a different story from the one she had given Stephanie. "But you told me you went out because you couldn't sleep and you wanted to—"

"I couldn't sleep because a bear was growling!" Marguerite said.

"But you said—" Stephanie began.

"I can't believe you, Stephanie! You're going to argue with Marguerite now?" Cynthia asked.

"You're the one who's supposed to go outside and check out strange noises! But, no, you were sound asleep," Cynthia said. "What if it *was* a bear? What if Marguerite was attacked?"

"That wouldn't happen," Stephanie said confidently.

"But it could have," Cynthia said. "Honestly, Stephanie, I think they made you a CIT a little too quickly. I think you need lots more training—you're obviously not ready for the job!" Cynthia took Marguerite's sleeping bag off her bed and threw it over her shoulder. "Come on, Marguerite—you're sleeping in my cabin tonight."

Tracey stepped in front of them. "No, she's not," she said. "Your little sister is fine here." She looked at Stephanie, and then at Marguerite. "I don't know why you ran off into the woods, but don't do it again. It could be dangerous, which is why you're not allowed to take off in the middle of the night."

Go, Tracey! Stephanie thought.

Cynthia and Marguerite went toward the door to say good-bye to each other. They whispered for a few seconds, and then Cynthia turned and glared at Stephanie.

"I still say *she's* responsible," she told Tracey. "I didn't want to say anything before, because I was trying to spare Stephanie's feelings. But the real reason Marguerite left is that she got into a fight with Stephanie—and she wanted to run away from camp!"

"What?" Tracey asked. "Is that true?"

Marguerite nodded, while Stephanie shook her head. "No," Stephanie said. "We didn't have a fight. Marguerite, how could you say that?"

"Okay, maybe not, but I *was* running away," Marguerite said.

"In your pajamas?" Tracey scoffed. "Look. I don't know what's going on here, but it's much too late to be playing games. Cynthia, please go back to your cabin. Marguerite, please wash up and get back into bed."

After they were gone, Tracey turned to Stephanie. "I'm not sure what that was all about, but it seems like you and Marguerite really don't get along. You're working on that, aren't you?"

"I'm trying really hard," Stephanie said. "But she has her mind made up against me." *And it's all thanks to the Flamingoes*, she said to herself.

"Well, keep trying. I don't want her to run off again," Tracey said.

"We absolutely didn't argue," Stephanie said. "And I don't think she was really running away."

"Maybe not, but she's still a problem," Tracey whispered. "You have to keep tabs on her and find a way to get through to her. Just . . . be more aware of your campers. That's all I ask," Tracey said.

"Sure," Stephanie said. "Of course."

And all I ask is that the Flamingoes leave me alone and quit making me look bad!

CHAPTER
10

◆ ◂ ◖ ◆

The next morning Stephanie stood on the end of the dock and stared at the lake. *I can't believe it. Another boat! Am I having the worst week, or what?*

She had been searching for the green canoe for ten minutes. She had already listened to a lecture from Keira. Now Mr. McCready had shown up!

"I just came down to prepare some things for Wild and Wacky Water Day." Mr. McCready set down a stack of signs he was carrying. "What's going on, Keira? You look upset."

"Remember how I told you we're having trouble keeping all the boats here?" Keira said. "Well, this is the third morning lately that one has drifted off. This is really getting out of control!

We're having a sort of epidemic of vanishing boats," Keira said. "I'm sorry, Mr. McCready—I don't know how it's happening. We have Stephanie on the job full-time, practically."

Mr. McCready pushed his hat back and scratched his forehead. "Stephanie, what explanation can you give me?" he asked.

Stephanie shrugged. "I don't know what to say. I've been so careful! I make sure the boats are all tied securely before dinner, and then I check them before lights-out." She shook her head. "It's so frustrating!"

"I agree," Mr. McCready said. "How can one boat come untied every night? It's as if someone's deliberately cutting them loose."

Stephanie shrugged. "That's what I think, too." She wouldn't tell Mr. McCready that she was afraid the "someone" might be Luke!

"Either way, the last thing we can afford is to lose a boat and have to replace it." Mr. McCready frowned. "I'm very concerned about this. Maybe we should ask someone else to take over—someone with more experience," he suggested to Keira.

"Please don't!" Stephanie said. "I promise, I'll get to the bottom of this."

"Stephanie, I don't want to replace you, but . . ." Keira pulled her hair back into a clip. "The fact is that it's been happening all week." A younger camper came up and whispered something in Keira's ear. "Excuse me," Keira said. "I need to run to the boathouse for a second."

"Just give me one more night," Stephanie pleaded with Mr. McCready when Keira was gone. "I—I have a plan. If it doesn't work, *then* you can take away this job. Because I promise you both—*I'm* not responsible for any of those boats drifting away. But I'm going to find out who is!"

Mr. McCready tied banners to the posts on the dock. "I'd like to believe you, Stephanie. But you know, this isn't the only problem I've heard about lately. Tracey and Heather came to my office after breakfast and told me how Marguerite Hansen ran off last night."

Stephanie's heart sank. Now Heather and Mr. McCready knew about her problems with Marguerite? Everything was making her look like the worst CIT ever!

Mr. McCready turned to Stephanie. "I know you're in a new job, and adjusting to being a CIT takes time. But if you really want a counseling job, you have to take it very seriously."

"I—I do," Stephanie said. "And I'm really dedicated to becoming a counselor someday."

"Well, first you'll need to prove that you can be more responsible," Mr. McCready said.

Why do I feel like I'm getting a report card? Stephanie kept smiling at Mr. McCready, but inside she was a bundle of nerves. *And it's full of F's?*

"You have to meet all the requirements of your job," Mr. McCready continued. "You have to look out for all your campers—and when one of them is difficult, you need to put in extra time, as much as it takes."

Stephanie nodded. "I've been trying really hard to get along with Marguerite. But I'll try harder."

"Good. And when you get a special assignment, like the one down here at the waterfront—you also need to put in extra time," Mr. McCready advised her.

"I will," Stephanie said. *Like tonight—on my stakeout!* "I promise, Mr. McCready—this is the last time you'll have to talk to me about this."

Mr. McCready smiled. "That's what I like to hear. Well, I'm off to make some more arrangements for tomorrow. Have a great day!"

Stephanie waved good-bye to him with a

cheery smile on her face. Now she was even more determined to catch whoever was untying the boats. *This is going to be my last rescue mission*, she thought as she headed to the boathouse to recruit a helper. She couldn't wait to hide out at the lake that night—and catch whoever was making her life miserable.

"Hey, Stephanie!" Max greeted her as he walked down the dock.

"Hi, Max," she said. "Feel like going for another boat trip this morning? It'll be very scenic—I promise. We might even tour the entire lake."

"Uh-oh. Another disappearing act?" Max made a face.

Stephanie nodded. "This one's a green canoe—I haven't even spotted it yet."

"What do we have to do, *weld* the boats to the dock?" Max joked. "Wait—I have an idea. Let's take them out of the water. Every night. You and I will carry each and every one to the boathouse, then bolt the door."

Stephanie smiled. "That might work, but are we strong enough?"

"You know, Stephanie, someone has to be doing this on purpose," Max said.

"I thought of that," Stephanie admitted. "But who?"

"I'd almost say it was Luke, if he hadn't been kicked out of camp already." He glanced nervously at Stephanie. "Sorry—was that totally out of line?"

"No. Well, maybe. I know it's not Luke, though," Stephanie said. *At least, I hope it's not.*

"Why are you so sure?" Max asked.

"I just am," Stephanie said. "He's gone, for one thing. And for another, why would he want to mess things up for me? We were . . . friends." *And something more.*

"True. Okay, then . . . forget friends. Do you have any enemies around here?" Max asked.

Stephanie thought of the night she'd bumped into Rene and Tiffany on her way back from the lake. She'd been so worried about their seeing Luke that she hadn't thought much about what they were doing. Did they cut a boat loose—just to get Stephanie in trouble? She wouldn't put it past them. But could they be pulling it off every night?

"Okay. Maybe you don't have any enemies," Max said while Stephanie was still thinking about the Flamingoes. "Maybe this is something completely weird, like aliens or something. After all, wild and wacky is the theme this week."

Stephanie laughed. "That has to be it. But why don't *you* tell Mr. McCready about the aliens landing at camp and stealing our boats?"

"Hey, speaking of Wild and Wacky Day . . . are you guys practicing today?" Max asked. "Because, you know, you'll need to practice a *lot* if you want to beat my team."

"Oh, really," Stephanie said.

Max nodded. "Charlie showed me the schedule of events. I found out that your cabin and my cabin are scheduled to race each other in the Battle of the Ten-Year-Olds."

"No way," Stephanie replied. "Wow. Too bad somebody has to lose. Too bad it'll have to be *you* guys."

"We're not losing," Max said. "In fact I'll make a bet with you. I bet . . ." He gazed out at the water. "I bet I can swim to the raft out there faster than you!" He pulled off his T-shirt and dove off the end of the dock into the water.

"No fair!" Stephanie shouted. Then she slipped out of her flip-flops, tossed her sweatshirt onto the dock and dove in after him. She surfaced and started swimming. The raft was only twenty yards away—she didn't have much time to catch him. She kicked her legs to power herself forward. Ahead of her, she could see Max's arms slice through the water. She kicked even harder and pulled herself with each crawl stroke. She got closer to Max—she was only half a body length behind him!

"Done!" Max touched the raft seconds before Stephanie. "You're fast."

"And *you* had a head start," Stephanie panted. "Want to race back?"

"Sure," Max said. "But let's hang out for a while first. You know, so you can recover." He grinned at her.

"As if I need to!" Stephanie climbed up the ladder onto the raft, while Max pulled himself over the side. They collapsed next to each other and stretched out under the bright morning sun.

"That felt great," Stephanie said with a sigh. "It's been a while since I really pushed myself."

"Wait until the contests tomorrow," Max said. "You can push yourself in eight different events."

"I'd like to, but I think I'm only doing the Silly Sailboat Race," Stephanie said.

"No way! Why?" Max asked.

Stephanie shrugged as she turned over onto her

stomach. "There's too much to do. Getting every-one ready for the race will be hard enough."

"Wait a second," Max said. "Your costumes must be a lot more complicated than ours. What's your theme?"

"I'm not telling," Stephanie said. "What if you stole it?" She pictured ten boys—including Max—dressed up as Famous Women in History and laughed.

"What? What's so funny?" Max demanded.

"Nothing," Stephanie said. Then she imagined Max wearing the Cleopatra costume—and cracked up all over again.

Max laughed and shook his head. "You're going to be so busy *laughing* that we'll cruise right by you!"

"Oh, no you won't," Stephanie said. "We're fast!"

"So are we. I'm competing in almost every-thing," Max said. "The marathon swim, the kayak sprint—"

"Still going for that all-around award?" Steph-anie asked.

Max nodded. "Since Luke isn't here, I might actually have a shot at it," he said.

"Well, good luck," Stephanie said. "Would you mind if I took a nap? Lying in the sun is so relaxing."

"I'll wake you up when it's time for us to race back," Max said.

"Sure you will," Stephanie said as she closed her eyes. "You'll dive in and then tell me it's time—I know you."

Max laughed. "Hey, anything to win a bet, right?"

Stephanie wished she were competing in all the events, like Max was. If Luke were still there, he'd probably win the award—again. Stephanie tried to picture Luke competing in the events and felt a pang of sadness when she realized how much she missed him. *I wonder if I'll ever see him again*, she thought.

Quit thinking that way! Stephanie scolded herself. *Luke is gone—you're with Max now.* She turned her head and looked over at Max. He was lying on his back and his eyes were closed. This was the perfect opportunity to beat him back to the docks!

She crept to her feet and made it to the edge of the raft. "Ready?" she said.

"Hey—no fair!" Max scrambled up beside her.

But Stephanie was already diving into the lake!

After her morning windsurfing class, Stephanie hurried back to her cabin and quickly changed out of her swimsuit into shorts and a T-shirt. She was meeting all of her best friends for lunch—she couldn't wait to tell them what a good time she'd had with Max.

On the way to the lodge, Stephanie stopped by the camp post office. She hoped there would be a letter from her family. She really missed them.

Inside, Rene, Tiffany, and Darah were standing at the open window. As Stephanie got closer, she saw they were putting stamps on a stack of post-cards.

"Excuse me." Stephanie stepped up to the window and smiled at the woman working there. "Is there anything for Stephanie Tanner?"

"I don't think so, but let me check," the woman behind the counter said. She sorted through a bas-ket marked "R-Z."

"Want us to send you a postcard, Stephanie?" Rene asked. "That way you'll get some mail."

Tiffany and Darah started laughing.

Stephanie turned to Rene with a bored expres-sion. "Yes, but who would want to get mail from you?"

"Aha! I was wrong," the woman said. "Here you are, Stephanie." She handed a small white envelope across the counter.

"Thank you. Looks like I won't be needing that postcard, you guys. But thanks for the offer," Stephanie said as she tapped the letter. She looked at the envelope. The handwriting looked sort of familiar, but there was no return address. She stared at the postmark. The letter had been mailed right here in town!

"Who's it from? Darcy?" Rene asked. "No, wait—you probably mailed it to yourself."

Stephanie tore open the envelope and stared at the sheet of paper. It was from Luke!

CHAPTER
11

Stephanie stared at the sheet of paper covered in Luke's handwriting. She couldn't believe it. Why was he writing to her? She took a deep breath and started reading.

Dear Stephanie,

I feel really badly about what happened the last time I saw you. I was only trying to help you get back to shore. Instead I got you into even more trouble with Heather. That wasn't what I wanted! What I really wanted was to talk to you.

You have no idea how much I miss you, and how lousy I feel about the way things turned out. I just can't let the summer go by without fixing it between us. I don't want you to be angry with me. I have to prove to you that I'm not the guy who trashed the lodge. And I don't know how I'll do it, but I'll try.

I want to see you for more than a few minutes at a time. We belong together, Stephanie. And I promise I'll see you very soon—maybe when you least expect it.

Luke

Stephanie stood outside on the post office steps and read the letter three times. She had never gotten such a romantic letter before. *We belong together*. Stephanie felt the same way.

Wait a second—what about Max? she thought. *I've been having a really good time with him. But I can't say I feel the same sort of connection with Max that I do with Luke. No matter how cute and funny Max is . . . it's just not the same!*

Stephanie hurried from the post office to the lodge. She and her friends had arranged to have lunch together, since the CITs had a free lunch once a week. Stephanie rushed into the dining room and spotted Allie, Darcy, Kayla, and Anna at a table in the far corner.

"You guys are not going to believe this,"

Stephanie announced as she sat down. "Guess what I got in the mail?" She held up the letter.

"Wait—don't tell me." Darcy peered over Stephanie's shoulders at the Flamingoes, who had just entered the dining room, too. "A postcard from the Flamingoes?"

"No." Stephanie scooted her chair closer to the table. "But they threatened to send me one."

"So who's it from—Michelle?" Allie asked.

Stephanie shook her head and grinned. "No offense to my little sister, but this is better. *Much* better."

"The suspense is killing me!" Kayla held up a plate of sandwiches. "Tell us who it's from right now or you won't get one of these."

"Hey, pass them over here," Allie said. "I'm starving!"

"And you—*spill*," Darcy urged as she tapped Stephanie on the arm with a fork.

Stephanie took a sip of cold pink lemonade. "The letter's from Luke!" she told everyone. "And it's really romantic."

"That is so cool—let me see!" Darcy said.

"What did he say?" Anna asked eagerly.

Allie didn't look nearly as excited. "Why is he even *writing* you?"

"Yeah, aren't you guys sort of history?" Kayla asked.

"No!" Stephanie shook her head. "I mean . . . yes. But maybe not."

"What does that mean?" Allie asked. "I thought you liked Max. You told me you thought he was great."

"I do like Max," Stephanie said slowly. "I mean, I think I do. But it's hard to explain. I just feel closer to Luke somehow. He even says it in his letter: It's like we belong together."

"What? He said *that*?" Darcy shrieked.

"Shh!" Stephanie warned her. "I don't want everyone to know he's writing me."

"Yeah, because you might get in trouble," Allie said. "You know, Steph, you're not supposed to be talking to Luke."

"Maybe not, but—"

"But what? Why do you want to have anything to do with him after what he did to the lodge?" Allie argued.

Stephanie tapped the envelope against the table. "I'm not convinced *he* did anything to the lodge. I mean, I don't think he's guilty. He's promised me, over and over, that he didn't have anything to do with it—"

"And you believe him?" Allie scoffed.

"Yes, I do," Stephanie said. She looked around the table at everyone. "You guys don't know Luke the way I do. He's not like that. And maybe I'm making a mistake, but he asked me to help him prove he's innocent. I'm thinking about helping him."

"If Luke is innocent . . . then who *is* responsible?" Anna wondered. "I mean, does he have any ideas? Do you?"

"But Luke's responsible," Allie insisted. "Don't you think the counselors and Mr. Davis checked everything out before they asked Luke to leave camp? I'm sure they had a pretty strong case."

"They could be wrong," Darcy mused as she picked up half a sandwich. "What if it was someone else? Someone who wanted to get rid of Luke for the summer—so they framed him?"

"I've thought about that," Stephanie said. "But who?"

"Luke might have been standing in this person's way," Darcy said. "And I don't want to say this because I know you guys like Max a lot. But I think it could have been Max who framed Luke."

"What? That's ridiculous!" Allie said.

"Is it?" Darcy said.

Anna laughed. "Darcy, you sound like one of those trial lawyers on TV shows."

"Sorry, but I've thought about it," Darcy said. "Luke was always the best at everything, right? And he and Max have been coming here for years. Luke always won everything. He's a better swimmer, a better water-skier—et cetera."

"So?" Kayla asked.

"So that's one reason Max would want Luke gone," Darcy said.

"I did think of that before—I mean, I knew they were both really competitive with each other," Stephanie said.

"And here's something else. I've seen the way Max looks at you, Steph. Even before you guys were dating, he totally had a crush on you," Darcy said.

"And that's wrong?" Allie scoffed.

"It is if Max set Luke up so that he could have Stephanie all to himself," Darcy said. "I mean, the only way Stephanie was going to break up with Luke was if he wasn't here anymore."

"Why do you have it in for Max?" Anna asked.

"I just don't trust him," Darcy said. "And you didn't used to, either," she reminded Stephanie.

"Remember when he kept warning you about Luke? He just wanted to make trouble and keep you guys apart."

"He definitely had the most to gain if Luke was kicked out of camp," Kayla said.

"I can't believe you guys!" Allie cried. "You have zero evidence. And you've already decided Max is behind all this? You have no proof!"

"When I think about it maybe I do have a funny feeling about him," Anna said. "Call it intuition—or whatever. I guess I don't trust Max, either."

"Well, I do," Allie insisted. "Don't you trust him, Stephanie?"

"Sure. I mean, of course I do," Stephanie said.

Except for this little voice inside me that keeps saying Luke couldn't have trashed the lodge. And if it isn't Max, then who else is there? He's the only one who had a motive to do it.

"I think you should definitely hear Luke out and try to find out who's behind all this," Anna said.

"I agree," Kayla said. "It can't hurt, right?"

"Sure it can," Allie said. "Because if Max knows you suspect him, he's going to be furious with you, Stephanie. Then when you find out you're wrong, he won't forgive you. It'll be all over between you guys. Do you really want that? All you've been talking about lately is how much fun it is to be with Max."

Darcy shook her head. "No, all she's been talking about lately is how much she misses Luke! I say give him another chance."

"You guys don't know Max like I do," Allie said. "He'd never do anything so devious and mean."

"I don't see how he could, either," Stephanie told her as she stared at Luke's letter. "But after everything that's happened, I don't know what to think anymore!"

"Tracey? I need to ask a favor," Stephanie said that night after everyone had gone to bed.

Tracey smiled as she brushed her hair. "Okay— what is it?"

"I need to leave for a little while," Stephanie said. "Actually, I might need to camp out tonight."

Tracey stopped brushing and stared at Stephanie. "What? Why? Is something wrong?"

"No! I mean, yes. Actually, there is—it's the disappearing boats," Stephanie said. "I'm convinced someone's taking them out at night and not tying them up properly. It's the only thing that makes sense. And I figure, the only way I can stop them—whoever it is—is by catching them red-handed."

"Well, a stakeout sounds like a good plan," Tracey said, nodding. "I feel kind of funny about you camping out there by yourself, though. How about if you hang out down there for an hour—then come back?" she suggested.

Stephanie frowned. "What if nothing happens in an hour?"

"Come back, check in with me—I'll be up late reading, as usual," Tracey said. "We'll decide whether you should go back."

"Okay. Deal," Stephanie agreed. It wasn't what she was hoping for. But considering how things had been going lately, she was grateful Tracey trusted her enough to let her go out after-hours.

Stephanie pulled on her red fleece jacket, waved to Tracey, and quietly slipped outside. She found a spot near the beach where she could sit on a tree stump, behind a large bush. Nobody would see her, but with the bright boathouse light, Stephanie could see the docks clearly.

Stephanie wrapped her arms around herself to

stay warm. She peered out at the lake. Small waves caught the light of the moon and sparkled as they moved. It was a breezy night. *Maybe someone will be out sailing*, she thought with a faint smile.

She listened hard for a boat on the lake, but heard nothing. As the minutes ticked by, Stephanie thought about the contests the next day and how much fun they'd be. She remembered Max saying he planned on winning the all-around title now that Luke was gone.

Is Darcy right? Did Max want to win so much that he had to get Luke to leave camp? She thought of how many times Max had arrived just in time to cheer her up, and how he'd kissed her on their hike. Max was too nice to be involved in framing someone.

All of a sudden Stephanie heard a rushing sound—like that of a boat moving on water. She parted two branches in front of her. She saw a canoe paddle being raised, and the clunking sound of a boat crashing into the docks.

Her eyes strained to focus. It was a canoe—with two boys in it.

"Watch it, Keith—you'll sink us!" a boy whispered as they knocked into another post.

Stephanie stared at them. *Keith? But who's with him?*

She didn't recognize the second voice.

Then Stephanie heard a familiar giggle and saw a flash of blond hair under the boathouse light. It was Tiffany—and Rene was with her!

CHAPTER
12

◆ ◂ ◆ ◆

Stephanie stared in shock. Tiffany and Rene were meeting boys secretly down by the beach. Maybe they'd done this before. They could even be the ones who had been taking the boats out at night.

"Tyler!" Tiffany called. She waved happily at him. "Be careful!"

That's the guy Tiffany was talking about, Stephanie realized. *The one who's supposed to be so cute.*

Stephanie couldn't wait a second longer. She stood up—and brushed against the bush that was hiding her. Its branches rustled.

"What was that?" she heard Keith say. He looked around the beach area with a panicked expression.

"I don't know—let's get out of here!" Tyler said. He started to back paddle as fast as he could.

"Hey, wait for us!" Tiffany cried as she rushed down to the water's edge.

"Yeah—what about our moonlight ride?" Rene demanded.

"Sorry. See you tomorrow," Keith whispered loudly.

"Good night!" Tyler waved his paddle in the air. "And remember—we were never here." The canoe disappeared into the darkness of the lake.

Stephanie waited until Rene and Tiffany had walked past her. Then she came out from behind the bush and jumped into the path. "Just so you know—I saw everything!" Stephanie told them.

Tiffany's eyes went wide, and she opened her mouth to scream.

Rene immediately clapped a hand over Tiffany's mouth. "Quiet! We'll get caught," she whispered fiercely.

Stephanie folded her arms in front of her and gazed at them with a smile. "You just *did*."

"You didn't see anything," Rene said quickly as she let Tiffany go. "You don't know anything!"

"Um . . . let me see. You were going out on the

lake after-hours. Without permission. You were going with boys from Camp Clearwater . . . I think that's *something*," Stephanie said. She wanted to enjoy every second of this.

"We were going out for a moonlight canoe ride. That's all," Tiffany said. "Aren't we allowed to enjoy nature?"

"No. Not when you're doing it on purpose to get me in trouble," Stephanie said.

"What?" Tiffany said.

"What are you talking about?" Rene asked.

"I think you guys have been taking boats out at night to meet your boyfriends!" Stephanie said. "And you didn't tie them up right when you got back, and I got in trouble every single morning afterward. I can't believe it was you guys, all along. When everyone finds out you've been sneaking out to Clearwater every night—"

"We haven't gone there at all! Not ever," Rene protested.

Stephanie wasn't convinced. "Somehow, I don't believe that," she said.

"We've *never* made it to the boys' camp," Tiffany said, pouting. "We tried a couple of times, but—"

"Tiffany!" Rene whispered harshly.

"Well, it's *true*. We did try," Tiffany said. "But the first night, we ran into you down here, so we had to turn around. Then when we went back later, I thought we were taking the sailboat, but there was no wind, only I didn't know that, so . . . anyway, we never went anywhere."

"Well, the boat did," Stephanie said. "And I totally got in trouble for it."

"The second night we tried to go there was that big thunderstorm," Rene said. "We turned back."

"And you were probably running to get out of the rain, so you didn't tie up the rowboat—"

"Yes, we did," Tiffany said. "Rene made me do it!"

Stephanie shook her head. She was sure Tiffany didn't know how to tie a knot in anything but a hair ribbon. "Look, maybe you never made it, but it's still breaking a huge camp rule—"

"No way," Rene said. "Not technically."

"Okay then, what about the *next* night?" Stephanie demanded. "When the canoe was missing the next morning?"

Tiffany put a hand over her mouth to cover a laugh. "Remember that, Rene? That was hilarious."

"It was not," Rene said. "You call leaping into the water and swimming for shore hilarious?"

She shook her head. "Tiffany forgot the paddles, but we didn't realize it until we were already ten feet from shore."

Stephanie brushed off her hands. "Well, that accounts for everything. Thanks for telling me the whole story. Now when I go to Mr. McCready to explain what's been going on, I'll have all the information I need." She plucked a burr off her jacket. "Well, see you, guys! I have to go start explaining why every single missing boat this week can be traced back to *you*." She turned toward the cabins.

"Wait a second," Rene said. She hurried up to Stephanie. "If I were you, I wouldn't do that."

"Oh, really?" Stephanie replied. "Why not? Because you might end up getting into serious trouble?"

"No, because *you* might," Rene said. "Because if you tell Heather or Mr. McCready or anyone what we've been doing, *I'll* tell him you and Luke Hayes have been meeting down here."

"What? But we haven't," Stephanie said.

A grin spread across Rene's face. "I saw the two of you together a few nights ago. There's no point denying it."

"You've got it all wrong. We never planned to meet," Stephanie said.

"But you did, anyway," Rene shot back. "In fact, you guys were standing right over . . . there. Isn't that right, Tiffany?"

"No," Tiffany said.

What? Is Tiffany going to stand up for me? Stephanie hoped.

"Actually, it was over there, by *that* tree." She pointed slightly to the right, then laughed.

"We only saw you get together with Luke once," Rene said. "I bet that wasn't the only time. But even if it was, it's still enough to get you in a lot more trouble than I'd be in. So if I were you, Stephanie, I wouldn't say a thing about seeing us down here tonight."

Stephanie glared at Rene. More than anything, she wanted to turn in Rene and Tiffany for taking the boats. They had nearly cost her the CIT job. But if she said anything about it, they'd bring up Luke's name and *that* would probably cost her the CIT job, too. She was stuck!

Rene had her hands on her hips and was glaring right back at Stephanie. Stephanie knew what that look meant: Rene was dead serious about this. If Stephanie even *thought* about going to Mr. McCready, Rene would find out about it.

"So, everything's settled, right?" Rene asked.

116

"Not quite," Stephanie said. "I have something else to say. If you guys ever take out another boat, I'll make sure someone else finds out about it. *They* can turn you in, even if I can't."

"What are you going to do? Have your friends spy on us?" Rene scoffed.

Stephanie grinned. "That's not a bad idea." There was nothing her friends would like more than helping her catch the Flamingoes red-handed!

CHAPTER
13

◆ ◂ ◗ ◆

Hey!" Anna put her fingers in her mouth and let out a loud whistle. "Nice costume, Steph!"

Stephanie laughed as she adjusted her red sequined bathing suit. "Well, I told you Esther Williams was glamorous."

"I love it," Anna said. "And it's so practical, too."

Stephanie shrugged as she adjusted the red bow in her hair. "I really want to be able to get in and out of our sailboat *fast*. This is a race, after all."

"I'm so glad it's not raining today!" Kayla stood on the docks. She was tying ribbons all over the springboard that would be used for the diving competition. "Can you imagine a *wet* Wild and Wacky Water Day?"

"It wouldn't be half as much fun," Stephanie said. "Even though we'll probably all end up getting soaked by the time we're through."

"After my belly flop? Everyone in the *audience* is going to be drenched," Darcy said.

Stephanie laughed. "I hope I'm around to see that. I have to time the Swim Medley Race, before the Silly Sailboat Race. At least there's a good breeze today! Maybe a little *too* good." She eyed the small whitecaps on the water.

Allie spray-painted a sign to show the end point for the kayak sprint. "All my campers are so psyched for today!"

"Mine, too." Stephanie's cabin was busy putting the final decorations on their small sailboat. She had just run over to say hello to her friends and to tell them what happened the night before—then she needed to get back!

"So did Rene say she planned on ruining your race today?" Darcy asked.

"No. I think I scared her off, actually," Stephanie said. "Since I caught her and Tiffany last night, she knows I'm watching her. And I told her *you* guys would all be watching her, too. Well, I'll see you later!"

"Good luck in your sailboat race!" Darcy called after her.

Stephanie waved and walked over to join Tracey and the girls from her cabin. They were adding brightly colored streamers to the mast.

"This looks great!" Stephanie said.

"I think we're almost done," Tracey said. "So you guys remember how the race works, right? Four of you will get dropped off on a raft over there by Clearwater." She pointed across the lake. "Four of you will stay on the docks. The first sailor leaves here and picks up one of you from the raft. When you get back here, you both get out and a new sailor gets in and heads across the lake again to fetch another sailor. I know we didn't have much time to practice, but since you're all taking sailing this summer, I have complete confidence in you!"

"Everyone remembers what order we sail in, right?" Stephanie asked.

Tracey cleared her throat. "Actually, I was just going to tell everyone that there's been a *slight* change," she said. "Vanessa's going to go first, instead of Marguerite."

"What?" Marguerite cried. "But I wanted to be first. And I'm a better—"

"You *are* a good sailor," Tracey interrupted her. "But so is Vanessa. And I want you to sail the anchor leg, which everyone knows is really important."

"But the CITs sail the anchor leg," Marguerite said.

"That's right—they do. But you'll sail to the raft alone, pick up Stephanie, and the two of you will finish together. And I know you two will finish strong."

Marguerite looked over at Stephanie and frowned.

Hey, this wasn't my idea! Stephanie wanted to tell her.

"I figured you guys might be able to bond if you did this together," Tracey told Stephanie a few minutes later. "You have to work together, sooner or later."

Stephanie nodded. "Good idea. I'm looking forward to it."

She couldn't help worrying about sailing with Marguerite, though. She could just see her refusing to hold the sail or steer—just because Stephanie asked her to.

"Here you are, girls!" Heather stopped the large motorboat beside one of the rafts that was the relay point for the Silly Sailboat Race. Stephanie spotted Max and three of his campers on a raft floating about ten feet away.

"Now, remember the rules!" Heather called.

Stephanie and her campers Debra, Ashley and Jessica stepped one at a time out of the motorboat and on to the raft. "Don't worry," Stephanie told her with a smile as she helped Ashley. "We've got it under control!"

"Sure you do!" Max called from his raft.

Stephanie turned to look at them. The boys were all wearing different baseball uniforms. All of them had baseball caps and team jerseys or T-shirts, and some even had baseball pants and cleats. They had put shiny black smudges under their eyes to shield their eyes from the sun.

"Maybe you think you're ready, but you're still going to lose," one of the boys yelled.

"We are *not*!" Ashley shouted over to them. "What kind of costumes do you call those, anyway?"

"Hey, at least we don't look like it's Halloween!" a boy yelled back. "Who are *you* supposed to be?"

"I'm Cleopatra," Debra said. "As if you couldn't tell."

"Who's Cleopatra?" Stephanie heard one boy ask another.

"I'm a famous Egyptian queen," Debra said as she flipped her black hair. *"Obviously."*

"Yeah. Right." He rolled his eyes. "And who are you?" He pointed to Jessica. "You have a cake pan on your head. Are you Betty Crocker? Or are you going to use that to bail out the sailboat—after you sink?"

"I'm Marie Antoinette," Jessica said proudly. "And may I present my friend, Amelia Earhart?"

Ashley took a bow while holding her goggles on her head to keep them from falling into the lake.

"Amelia Earhart's plane was never found," another boy said. "Maybe your sailboat will get lost."

"Maybe *you'll* get lost!" Ashley shouted back at him.

"Pipe down, everyone. Look—they're starting!" Max pointed across the lake.

Stephanie spotted Loon Cabin's sailboat immediately. The multicolored sail looked terrific in the bright sun on the lake. Sailing right next to it was a boat with a sail decorated like a baseball diamond.

Vanessa was off to a good start. When she neared the raft they were on, everyone from Loon Cabin started jumping up and down and screaming.

"All right, Vanessa!" Debra yelled.

"Way to go!" Stephanie called.

Max's cabin's sailboat was only two seconds behind Vanessa's. When they reached the two rafts, both sailors pulled up carefully and waited. Debra tried to jump into the boat, but she tripped on her long gold dress and nearly fell into the lake.

"Sorry, Cleopatra!" Max called over as his sailboat smoothly executed the change and sailed back toward the other raft.

"We're losing time—hurry!" Ashley screamed at Debra as she rearranged herself in the boat.

"We're going, we're going!" Vanessa called over her shoulder.

Stephanie watched her team lose some valuable yards to Max's boat as they headed toward Camp Sail-Away. "Come on, you guys!" she rooted. "We can't let them beat us!"

"Get used to it," Max said as his team traded sailors on the opposite side of the lake. "We're too far ahead—you'll never catch us!"

"Yes, we will," Stephanie called back. "Won't we, guys?"

Ashley and Jessica screamed their support for Tammy as she sailed closer. She was dressed as Wilma Rudolph, the track star, in shorts and a sleeveless T-shirt, with a pair of running shoes loosely looped around her shoulders. But she wasn't going very fast—they were falling too far behind. Jessica jumped into the sailboat, and Tammy made a tight, clean turn, but they still lagged behind the boys.

"Come on, Richard!" Max yelled as his next sailor approached the raft.

Anne came along about thirty seconds later. She and Ashley were the next team. *It'll be up to me and Marguerite*, Stephanie realized as she watched both teams make the final exchange on the other side of the lake.

"So, Stephanie. What was our bet again?" Max teased once he and Stephanie were the only ones left on each raft. "Something about how if your team loses, you have to wait on me, hand and foot, for the rest of the summer?"

"Hardly!" Stephanie said with a laugh. "First of all, we never made that bet. And second, who says you're going to win?"

Max checked his watch. "How about the fact that our boat is at least a minute ahead of yours?"

"Stop looking at your watch—look at the lake," Stephanie told him, excited. "Marguerite is really gaining on your guy!"

"What?" Max sputtered. "But that's impossible. Tony's our best sailor—besides me."

"And Marguerite's *our* best sailor," Stephanie retorted. She adjusted the hat on her head. "So look out, because here she comes!" She grinned as she saw the sparkly silver gloves Marguerite was wearing with her Princess Diana costume. She had fake gemstones glued to a tiara on her head and a long ice-blue gown. The sleeves billowed out as she sailed along.

The wind had picked up a little, and both sailboats were cruising right along at top speed. Marguerite was gaining on Tony every second. Stephanie rubbed her hands together. She was so excited! They actually had a chance to win this thing.

And I know Marguerite and I can do this together, she thought. *We both want to win!*

"Go, Marguerite!" she yelled as the two boats approached the rafts. Marguerite was only a few boat lengths behind Tony.

Tony pulled up beside Max, and Max got into the sailboat. "Bye, Stephanie!" he shouted as they made the turn to sail off.

Just as they were heading out, Marguerite was coming in. She turned the boat upwind to stop going forward so she wouldn't crash into the raft. She nearly bumped right into Max and Tony!

"Watch where you're going!" Max shouted at her.

Marguerite pushed the tiller in the opposite direction. She veered away from them—and missed the raft completely!

"Come back!" Stephanie called to her.

Marguerite turned again. This time the wind caught the sail and sent it swinging over her head.

"Duck!" Stephanie yelled.

Marguerite ducked, but not fast enough. The boom hit her shoulder—and she went flying off the boat into the lake.

"Help!" Marguerite screamed as she went underwater. The long skirt on her costume floated up to the surface. But Marguerite didn't!

Stephanie didn't waste a second. She dove into the water to rescue her!

CHAPTER
14

◆ ◀ ◾ ◆

Stephanie surfaced and quickly located Marguerite. Then she started swimming as hard as she could toward her. She saw Marguerite's arms flailing above her head. She was struggling just to stay afloat!

Where's her life jacket? Stephanie wondered. Then she realized that a life jacket was floating in the lake. It must have come off when Marguerite fell in. Stephanie would have to remind Marguerite to keep her life jacket fastened—otherwise it was no use. But that would be later—much later. Right now she needed to get her back into the boat.

Marguerite was a good swimmer—Stephanie

had seen her down at the lake. But she was wearing a long costume, and her shoulder was hurt. She didn't stand a chance, unless Stephanie got to her!

Good thing she's not too far away, Stephanie thought as she pushed ahead. She was having a hard time swimming fast herself—the waves were choppy.

She glared at Max's sailboat as it disappeared toward the other shore. Why hadn't he come back to help them? He wasn't even looking to see if Marguerite was okay. *He had to have heard her yell for help!* she thought.

Stephanie finally reached Marguerite. She was coughing and sputtering, trying to keep her head above water. Stephanie crooked her arm around Marguerite's neck and tried towing her toward the boat. But the waves were quickly turning into whitecaps, and Marguerite felt so heavy with her waterlogged clothes. Stephanie wasn't making any progress.

"What are you doing?" Marguerite asked. When she spoke, she took in another gulp of water. She started coughing again. Then she began fighting against Stephanie and tried to break free.

"Don't talk," Stephanie said. "And quit moving. I'll get you back to the boat." She looked up from her task—and saw the boat had drifted at least twenty feet away! Now they were stuck halfway between the raft and the sailboat.

We're not close enough to either, Stephanie realized. Panic surged through her. *We might not make it!*

She heard a low humming sound behind her and turned around. A motorboat was approaching them! She heaved a giant sigh of relief when she saw who was driving the boat.

"Need a hand?" Luke shouted.

"Take Marguerite!" Stephanie cried. The motorboat pulled up to within a few yards of the girls, and Luke cut the motor. Stephanie dragged Marguerite the short distance.

"Here, let me—" Luke struggled to get a grip under Marguerite's shoulders. "Let go, Steph, I've got her!" He reached down and expertly pulled Marguerite into the motorboat. "Are you okay?" he asked as he helped her sit down.

Marguerite coughed more water out of her lungs, then nodded.

"You can breathe all right? Are you hurt anywhere?" Luke asked.

"My shoulder." Marguerite winced.

"The camp nurse will look at your shoulder as soon as we get back to camp, okay?" Luke told Marguerite. "Just try to relax. Take deep breaths. We'll get you there in just another minute."

Then Luke turned to Stephanie. "Now, how about you? Did you want a ride, or did you want to swim back across?" he teased as he leaned over the boat.

"Please?" Stephanie held her hand up to him.

Luke took both her hands and helped her climb into the boat. Stephanie threw her arms impulsively around Luke. "I'm so glad you came along! I didn't know what we were going to do. You're the best!" She hugged him tightly.

Luke took a step back and grinned. "Hey, if I knew you were going to do that, I would have rescued you days ago."

Stephanie felt herself blush. She grabbed a towel from the stern and wrapped it around Marguerite's shoulders. "How are you doing?" she asked.

"Okay," Marguerite said. "I don't look like a princess anymore."

"I think your tiara sunk. Sorry. But if it makes you feel better, you can laugh at me." Stephanie glanced down at her soaked, sparkling swimsuit.

"You guys both look great," Luke told them.

"Well, at least we're okay," Marguerite said. "Thanks to you. I don't actually care about my costume much right now!"

"Me either," Stephanie agreed. She turned to Luke. "You really saved the day. How can I thank you enough?"

"Well . . . maybe you'll believe me now when I say I didn't trash the lodge," Luke said. "Because isn't it obvious that I have nothing against this camp, or anybody at this place?"

Stephanie looked into Luke's eyes. He had come to her and Marguerite's rescue so swiftly. He wanted her to trust him again. Maybe now she finally could.

Stephanie took a deep breath and nodded. "I do believe you," she said.

Luke reached for Stephanie's hands. "So you'll help me prove I'm innocent?"

Stephanie nodded as she squeezed his hand. "Definitely."

"Yes!" Luke gave Stephanie a hug. "Then let's get you guys back to camp—I'm sure everyone's worried about you. Someone can come back for the sailboat later." He started the motor up and raced the engine as they headed for shore.

"I'm really sorry, Stephanie," Marguerite said as they both looked at the crowd waiting for them.

"It's not your fault," Stephanie told her. "Accidents happen. And besides, I think their boat was too close to yours."

"I wasn't talking about the race. I was talking about how I've been giving you such a hard time," Marguerite said. "It was all my sister's fault. She said she didn't like you, so I didn't like you, either. I never should have listened to her. You're the best counselor at camp!"

"Thanks," Stephanie said as she put her hand on Marguerite's shoulder. "But that's best CIT, actually." She winked at Marguerite as they came to a stop at the end of the docks.

A cluster of friends and counselors rushed up to them as they stepped out of the boat.

A shrill whistle pierced the air. "Come on, everyone—stand back!" Mr. McCready said. "We can't all be on the dock at once! Let's move this welcome party to the beach—now!"

"Luke! Nice going!" Charlie, a counselor at the boys' camp, called out to Luke, who hadn't gotten out of the boat. "Way to be in the right place at the right time."

"Nice rescue!" someone else added.

On the beach Stephanie's friends surrounded her and gave her a group hug. Then everyone from Loon Cabin came up and hugged both her and Marguerite.

Cynthia pushed her way through the crowd to the front. "Marguerite, are you okay?"

"I'm fine," Marguerite said. "Stephanie came to the rescue, so . . ." She looked up at Cynthia and shrugged. "Sorry, but she's not as bad as you said. In fact, she practically saved my life out there. Then Luke happened to show up and he pulled me into the boat—"

"Lucky for you guys Luke was out on the lake," Cynthia said.

"I know," Stephanie agreed.

Cynthia looked at her and smiled. "Thanks, Stephanie. I owe you *and* Luke a lot for rescuing Marguerite."

"You're welcome," Stephanie told her. "I'm really glad we were both there!"

"How come the boys' team didn't stop?" Darcy asked. She turned to Max, who was standing a few feet behind Stephanie. "If you guys had turned around to help, instead of going on with the race, *you* could have saved Marguerite. I'm sorry, but I think that was totally irresponsible of you!"

Stephanie was a little shocked by Darcy's out-burst. For some reason, Darcy really didn't like Max. But Stephanie had to admit that as much as she did like him, she felt disappointed in him now, too.

"It was a race," Max said. "We couldn't stop or we'd—"

"Lose?" Darcy interrupted. "Big deal! It's only a silly race. That's the name of it, okay?"

Except that Max wanted to win the all-around title, Stephanie thought. *Is winning more important to him than anything? Even when someone's in danger?*

"Look, Darcy, you're way off base here," Max retorted. "Marguerite didn't fall out of the boat because of me. It was Luke's fault. He came speeding up in his motorboat. His motor caused a huge wake, and Marguerite couldn't handle the waves. That's why she tipped over—"

"You're the reason she fell into the water. You nearly ran her down," Stephanie said. "And Luke wasn't even there until *after* that happened—"

"That's not true!" Rene pushed her way through the crowd to the front. "Stephanie planned to meet Luke out there during the race. He was there talk-ing to her the whole time!"

"What?" Ashley said. "He was not! I was there and I never saw Luke."

"That's right," Stephanie said.

"Then he came up afterward," Rene said. She gazed around at the crowd. "Big deal. You've still been meeting him in secret ever since he left camp!"

CHAPTER
15

◆ ◂ ▸ ◆

Stephanie was stunned. She couldn't believe Rene would announce she'd been seeing Luke in front of the whole camp!

"Stephanie, is that true?" Mr. McCready asked. "Look—why don't you all come over here, so we can continue this conversation in private?" He moved toward the boathouse.

Stephanie followed him. She was so surprised she couldn't speak at first. *How should I answer?* she wondered. *I never planned to meet Luke—but it's true I've seen him a few times.*

"Yes, of course it's true." Rene marched up to Mr. McCready's side. "Not only did she *plan* to meet Luke today on the lake, but Tiffany and I saw her and Luke together down here one night. *Late* one night—after lights-out! And then there was the *letter* Stephanie got from Luke—"

"What were you doing, reading over my shoulder?" Stephanie demanded.

"Since when is it a crime to get a letter from someone?" Darcy interjected.

"Yeah," Anna said. "That's not against camp rules."

"No, it's not, but what about meeting Luke after-hours?" Mr. McCready asked. "That's very serious, Stephanie."

"I came down to the lake to check the boats," Stephanie said. "And Luke was here, but it wasn't a plan. Anyway, why don't you ask Rene why she saw me that night?" Stephanie turned to Rene. "Tell Mr. McCready why you were down here."

Rene glared at Stephanie. She didn't say a word.

Stephanie turned back to Mr. McCready. "Rene and Tiffany were going to take a boat over to the boys' camp to meet their boyfriends. Only they're not very good at tying knots. That's why a boat was missing every morning!"

"I untied the sailboat by mistake, okay?"

Tiffany said. "Then Rene told me we couldn't sail at night because there wasn't any wind."

Rene swatted Tiffany on the arm. "That's not what happened. We didn't try to take a boat—"

"No, you tried to take three boats," Stephanie interrupted. "Three separate times!"

"Look, it—it's not my fault," Rene stammered. "He was the one who told us to steal the boats!" She pointed at Keith, who was standing on the edge of the beach crowd.

"What? This wasn't my idea!" Keith said as he marched over.

"Yes, it was. You said it would be fun to go canoeing under the moon, and—"

"That is a total lie," Keith said. "You guys were the ones who insisted on coming over to meet us. I only mentioned it once—"

"Then how come you came over to meet us last night?" Rene demanded.

While they argued, Max came up to Stephanie. She wasn't sure she even wanted to talk to him, after the way he'd acted. Who sailed away when someone was struggling to stay afloat in the middle of a lake?

Maybe Darcy's right. Maybe Max did want Luke to get kicked out of camp—because he couldn't stand coming in second all the time!

139

"Stephanie? Have you really been meeting Luke?" Max asked. He looked so hurt that for a second, Stephanie felt guilty.

"No," Stephanie insisted. "Well, not on purpose, anyway," she added.

Max still looked upset. Stephanie almost felt sorry for him—except that he'd just been a complete jerk about the sailboat race.

"I thought you guys were history," Max said. "I mean, you are, aren't you? I thought you and I—"

"I'm not sure what's going on with me and Luke," Stephanie cut him off. "But I do know that I believe in him."

Max's face fell. "You're kidding."

Stephanie shook her head. "Nope."

"This whole thing is very confusing," Mr. McCready said. He walked back down the docks toward Luke. The entire group followed.

Stephanie held her breath. What was Luke going to say? Would Mr. McCready even consider recommending that the boys' camp let him come back, once he found out Luke had sneaked back to see her?

"Luke? Before you go," Mr. McCready said. "Can you shed some light on the situation?"

"Yes. What do you have to say for yourself?"

Heather demanded. She had just pulled up in the camp motorboat. She was towing the Loon Cabin sailboat behind her.

"First of all, I know no one believes me yet, but I really didn't damage the lodge that night. But more important, Stephanie *never* made a plan to meet with me," Luke explained.

"She didn't?" Heather asked as she docked the motorboat and got out.

"No. I came by to find her," Luke said. "Maybe that was wrong, but I just had to see her. And both the times that I ran into her on the lake were complete coincidences. You know our house is down there, and I'm on the lake a lot, even if I'm not at camp anymore."

"Yes, we realize you're close by," Mr. McCready said. "And we knew that could cause problems— like today during the race."

"But Luke didn't cause a problem!" Marguerite said. "He came to my rescue. He saved me!"

"Marguerite's right," Stephanie said. "I was trying to swim back to the raft with Marguerite when Luke drove up. We didn't see him before then."

"That doesn't mean his boat wasn't there—" Max said.

"What is this, a trial?" Stephanie scoffed. "Come on, Max. Just admit that you were sailing too close—"

Heather blew her whistle. "Time out! This isn't getting us anywhere."

"I think we've heard enough," Mr. McCready declared. He turned to Luke and clapped him on the back. "Thanks again for showing up at the right time. But if you wouldn't mind—"

"No problem," Luke said with a nod. "I'll be going."

"Heather and I need to talk this over and decide what to do," Mr. McCready said. "You—" He pointed to Stephanie, Rene, Max, Tiffany, Keith, and Tyler. "*Don't* go anywhere."

Stephanie wandered over to Luke's side. She didn't want to say good-bye. She wished Luke were coming back to camp. She didn't want to let him out of her sight! They stood beside his motorboat. Stephanie didn't know what to say.

Luke took her hand and squeezed it tightly. "I wish I didn't have to go. I hate leaving you— especially when things are so up in the air!"

Stephanie looked into his eyes. "But they're not. I mean, not between us."

"Really?" Luke asked.

Stephanie nodded. "I'm sorry I was so mad at you."

Luke shrugged. "It's okay. You were probably right. I shouldn't have sneaked into camp to see you."

"No," Stephanie agreed. She smiled at him. "But I'm glad you did. So . . . will you do it again?" she asked.

"I'll see you soon," Luke promised. "Somehow. I will. We'll find a way."

They gave each other a long hug. Stephanie wanted to stay in Luke's arms forever.

There was a blast of a bullhorn, and she nearly jumped.

"We've reached our decision, Stephanie!" Heather announced. "Please return!"

Luke and Stephanie broke apart. "Heather calls . . ."

"Bye, Stephanie. I'll miss you!" Luke called as he hopped into his boat.

"I'll miss you, too," Stephanie said with an awkward wave.

Luke drove off, and Stephanie walked back to the docks.

"We've come to some decisions," Mr. Mc-Cready said when Stephanie rejoined the group. "Decisions we don't like to make!"

"Mr. M is quite upset by all this," Heather announced. "So I'll go ahead and tell you the bad news. I'm afraid we're going to have to put some of you on probation."

"Probation?" Tiffany asked. "What's that?"

Stephanie was too busy worrying about her future at camp to even listen to Heather's answer. Whatever it was, "probation" didn't sound good.

"The following CITs and campers are on probation," Heather continued. "Which means that one more mistake and you forfeit your summer at camp—with no refund."

"Why doesn't she just get *on* with it!" Darcy muttered under her breath.

"They won't put you on probation," Kayla said. "You didn't do anything wrong, Steph."

Heather cleared her throat. "Okay. Rene and Tiffany? You disobeyed camp rules, at least once and probably more than that. You're on probation," Heather said.

"What!" Rene cried. "But you have no proof—"

"And, Keith, you and Tyler are also on probation," Heather said. "We'll confer with Mr. Davis, but the way we see it, you were out at night without permission as well."

Stephanie looked at Keith. He was glaring at Rene.

"I have a feeling that little romance is over," Darcy said with a chuckle.

"Max, you're not on probation," Heather said. "But we'd like you to review water safety rules in depth. And we've disqualified you from today's race results."

"I *didn't* get in her way," Max muttered.

"Is that it?" Allie whispered. "Stephanie, they didn't mention your name. That means—"

"And, Stephanie, as far as you're concerned . . ." Heather went on.

Allie reached for Stephanie's hand and squeezed it. Stephanie squeezed back. She needed all the support she could get right then.

"Not only did you disobey camp rules by seeing Luke after he was banned from camp, you saw him even after I specifically warned you not to," Heather said. "I'm sorry, Stephanie. I know you were just getting started, but you'll have to give up your CIT position."

"No way!" Marguerite cried. "You can't do that to her."

"Stephanie's a great CIT," Debra added. "We don't want her to leave our cabin!"

"I'm sorry, girls. That's the way it has to be," Mr. McCready said.

Stephanie's eyes filled with tears. She was touched by the way her campers were standing up for her. But it wouldn't change Heather and Mr. McCready's minds.

How had everything gone so wrong? One minute she had won the CIT test and had a great new boyfriend. The next minute Luke was gone from camp and she was no longer a CIT!

"It means we'll be short one CIT again," Heather said.

"I could do it," Tiffany volunteered. "I took that test and did okay—"

"You're on *probation*," Heather reminded her. "I don't think so!"

"I'm sorry our Wild and Wacky Water Day had to end on such a bad note," Mr. McCready said. "It was really a wonderful day and there were lots of terrific performances. Heather, do you have the list of winners?"

While they announced the race results to the crowd, Stephanie's friends surrounded her.

"Stephanie, this is awful!" Anna said. "You're a great CIT."

"How could they do this?" Kayla asked.

"It's all because of Rene," Darcy said angrily.

"Stephanie? Say something," Allie urged. "Are you okay?"

"Don't you guys want to listen to the contest results?" Stephanie asked.

"Who *cares* about a stupid belly flop contest?" Allie said. "This is your summer, Stephanie. And the Flamingoes are trying to ruin it!"

Stephanie didn't say anything. She was busy thinking about everything that had happened that afternoon. Maybe she was no longer a CIT—but Luke still lived nearby. Now she'd have more time to spend proving his innocence. She'd show everyone how wrong they were about him!

The sailboat accident flashed through Stephanie's mind. She and Luke made such a good team. Kissing him felt so right to her!

"Steph? Are you still with us?" Darcy waved a hand in front of Stephanie's face.

"What are you thinking about?" Anna asked.

"Don't get mad at me," Stephanie said. "But I was thinking about Luke."

"I figured. Sorry." Kayla put an arm around Stephanie's shoulder.

"And I'm sorry I told you to go out with Max

instead," Allie said. "Boy, did he act like a jerk today!"

"Speaking of jerks." Rene stood in front of Stephanie.

"Here's one now!" Darcy said. "Ta-da!"

"I was talking about *her*." Rene glared at Stephanie. "It's all your fault I've been put on probation. I can't believe you told everyone about our trying to sneak over to the boys' camp!"

"I wouldn't have," Stephanie replied, "if you hadn't announced that I was making secret plans to see Luke."

"Yeah, you're acting like Stephanie's the one who started all this," Anna said. "You accused her first!"

"That doesn't matter," Rene said. "What matters is that *I'm* on probation now. But you know what? I'm going to ruin your summer the way you've ruined mine!"

"What are you talking about? You already *did*. You're the one who made me lose my CIT job!" Stephanie retorted.

"That wasn't my fault, and you know it," Rene said. "But thanks to you telling everyone about how I met Keith, they're going to be watching me constantly."

"They should," Darcy said. "Because you're usually up to something."

Rene frowned at her. "I'm sure you're happy, because Keith is furious with me now. I'll never go out with him again."

"Why would you want to?" Anna scoffed. "He's sort of a jerk. Oh, wait—that means you have something in common."

Rene turned to Stephanie and narrowed her eyes. "Look, I know you think you got away with something here. So let me just give you a piece of information. *I* know who trashed the lodge—and I know it wasn't Luke."

"What?" Stephanie cried. "What do you mean, you know who did it? Did *you* do it?"

"I'm not telling," Rene said. "Why should I?"

"Because if Luke didn't do it, clearing his name would be the right thing to do," Stephanie argued. "Please—tell me who did!"

"I'm not helping you with anything," Rene said. "Come on, Tiffany—let's get out of here." They started walking away.

As Rene's news sank in, Stephanie felt a rush of excitement. Maybe she was no longer a CIT, but at least she knew Luke really was innocent. And Rene knew who the culprit was!

Maybe now I can finally figure out who trashed the lodge—and got Luke kicked out of camp for something he didn't do! Stephanie thought excitedly. *And when I do, Luke can come back to camp, and we'll be together again . . . this time for good!*

WIN A $500 SHOPPING SPREE AT THE WARNER BROTHERS STUDIO STORE!

FULL HOUSE™ C L U B

Stephanie

1 Grand Prize: A $500 shopping spree at the Warner Brothers Studio Store

----

Complete entry form and send to: Pocket Books/ "Full House Club Stephanie Sweepstakes" 1230 Avenue of the Americas, 13th Floor, NY, NY 10020

NAME _____ BIRTHDATE ___/___/___

ADDRESS _____

CITY _____ STATE _____ ZIP _____

PHONE (_____) _____

PARENT OR LEGAL GUARDIAN'S SIGNATURE *(required for entrants under 18 years of age at date of entry.)*

_____

See back for official rules.

Pocket Books/ "Full House Club Stephanie Sweepstakes"
Sponsors Official Rules:

No Purchase Necessary.

Enter by mailing this completed Official Entry Form (no copies allowed) or by mailing a 3" x 5" card with your name and address, daytime telephone number and birthdate to the Pocket Books/ "Full House Club Stephanie Sweepstakes", 1230 Avenue of the Americas, 13th Floor, NY, NY 10020. Entry forms are available in the back of Full House Club Stephanie #10: Truth or Dare (6/00), #11: Summertime Secrets (7/00) and #12: The Real Thing (8/00), on in-store book displays and on the web site SimonSaysKids.com. Sweepstakes begins 6/1/00. Entries must be postmarked by 8/31/00 and received by 9/15/00. Sponsors are not responsible for lost, late, damaged, postage-due, stolen, illegible, mutilated, incomplete, or misdirected or not delivered entries or mail or for typographical errors in the entry form or rules or for telecommunications system or computer software or hardware errors or data loss. Entries are void if they are in whole or in part illegible, incomplete or damaged. Enter as often as you wish, but each entry must be mailed separately. Winner will be selected at random from all eligible entries received in a drawing to be held on or about 9/25/00. The Winner will be notified by phone.

Prizes: One Prize: A $500 shopping spree at the Warner Brothers Studio Store. (retail value: $500).

The sweepstakes is open to legal residents of the U.S. (excluding Puerto Rico) and Canada (excluding Quebec) ages 6-10 as of 8/31/00. Proof of age is required to claim prize. Prize will be awarded to the winner's parent or legal guardian. Void wherever prohibited or restricted by law. All federal, state and local laws apply. Simon & Schuster, Inc., Parachute Publishing, Warner Bros. and their respective officers, directors, shareholders, employees, suppliers, parent companies, subsidiaries, affiliates, agencies, sponsors, participating retailers, and persons connected with the use, marketing or conduct of this sweepstakes are not eligible. Family members living in the same household as any of the individuals referred to in the preceding sentence are not eligible.

Prize is not transferable and may not be substituted except by sponsors, in the event of prize unavailability, in which case a prize of equal or greater value will be awarded. The odds of winning the prize depend upon the number of eligible entries received.

If the winner is a Canadian resident, then he/she must correctly answer a skill-based question administered by mail.

All expenses on receipt and use of prize including federal, state and local taxes are the sole responsibility of the winner. Winner's parents or legal guardians may be required to execute and return an Affidavit of Eligibility and Publicity Release and all other legal documents which the sweepstakes sponsors may require (including a W-9 tax form) within 15 days of attempted notification or an alternate winner may be selected.

Winner or winner's parents or legal guardians on winner's behalf agree to allow use of winner's name, photograph, likeness, and entry for any advertising, promotion and publicity purposes without further compensation to or permission from the entrant, except where prohibited by law.

Winner and winner's parents or legal guardians agree that Simon & Schuster, Inc., Parachute Publishing and Warner Bros. and their respective officers, directors, shareholders, employees, suppliers, parent companies, subsidiaries, affiliates, agencies, sponsors, participating retailers, and persons connected with the use, marketing or conduct of this sweepstakes, shall have no responsibility or liability for injuries, losses or damages of any kind in connection with the collection, acceptance or use of the prize awarded herein, or from participation in this promotion.

By participating in this sweepstakes, entrants agree to be bound by these rules and the decisions of the judges and sweepstakes sponsors, which are final in all matters relating to the sweepstakes. Failure to comply with the Official Rules may result in a disqualification of your entry and prohibition of any further participation in this sweepstakes.

The first name of the winner will be posted at SimonSaysKids.com or the first name of the winner may be obtained by sending a stamped, self-addressed envelope after 9/31/00 to Prize Winners, Pocket Books "Full House Club Stephanie Sweepstakes," 1230 Avenue of the Americas, 13th Floor, NY, NY 10020.

TM & © 2000 Warner Bros.

2808-01 pg. 2 of 2